DREAM GIRL

DREAM GIRL

Joy Holley

TE HERENGA WAKA
UNIVERSITY PRESS

Te Herenga Waka University Press
Victoria University of Wellington
PO Box 600 Wellington
teherengawakapress.co.nz

A catalogue record is available at the National Library
of New Zealand.

ISBN 9781776920846

Printed in Singapore by Markono Print Media Pte Ltd

For all my girls

CONTENTS

Mission Strawberry   9

You Are Now Entering
the Grotto of the Prophetess   28

The Heart-Shaped Bed   37

Rat Trap   53

Girls in the Tunnel   71

Fruit   76

Compatibility Report   99

Urban Foraging   107

Material Girl   116

Moral Delinquency
in Children and Adolescents   122

Cottagewhores   139

Ghost Story   142

Nightmare Girl   164

Pets   166

Blood Magic   174

Manifesto   197

School Spirit   204

Notes and Acknowledgements   238

MISSION STRAWBERRY

Mission Strawberry was my idea. I had seen a place on Facebook about two hours' drive away where you could pick your own strawberries over summer, and I had a strong feeling that Wallace would be into this. Strawberries were one of the few foods the two of us agreed on: delicious. Also, Wallace had a car. Asking them to drive us would seem more like asking them a favour than asking them on a date.

When I told Wallace about the strawberry farm, their whole face lit up. 'Yesss,' they said, with hushed fervour.

I wished I could take a photo of the way they were looking at me, to analyse with Celeste later on.

Actually making Mission Strawberry happen was more difficult. We worked on different days, and Wallace was vague and flaky when I tried to make plans over Messenger. When we finally locked in a Saturday, they asked, 'Should I invite Celeste and the other flatmates?'

I had known they would ask this question, but still hoped they wouldn't. I typed and backspaced multiple replies, then said, 'Yeah sure.'

—

The days leading up to Mission Strawberry were a blur of fog and rain. The weather report promised a golden circle of sun for Saturday, but this seemed unlikely.

I slept over at the flat on Friday night. Celeste and I often had sleepovers: I had known her much longer than Wallace or the other flatmates. Celeste knew my intentions for Mission Strawberry and had agreed that if Alex and Sophie couldn't come, she would cancel too. Alex had wanted to come so much she swapped her Saturday shift to Sunday, and Sophie had already made bread for the drive. A part of me hoped the weather would be bad so we would have to postpone the mission, but I also knew it could take months to find another day that worked for just me and Wallace. Strawberries would be out of season by then. There was always a chance Sophie's boyfriend would call her last minute saying she wasn't allowed to go. Maybe Alex would come down with a vomiting bug overnight.

When Celeste opened the curtains, the weather was perfect.

I got out of bed and put my bra on—inspecting my neck in Celeste's mirror. The love bites from last week had faded, but now there was a scattering of new ones.

'Can I borrow your turtleneck?'

'Of course. Sorry about that.' She touched her finger to the biggest love bite. It was just under my jaw: a constellation of purple dots.

'It's all good,' I said. 'They never notice.'

Celeste took a black top out of her drawer. 'It's merino. You're gonna boil.'

'I'll manage.'

She passed it to me, then pointed at another mark on my neck. 'This one looks like a heart.'

I paused, my arms halfway into the top. 'Does that mean we're in love?'

We both laughed. I got out my make-up bag and started brushing out my eyebrows. I never wore much make-up, but I always made sure I looked perfect before seeing Wallace. They didn't know anything about make-up, and I suspected they didn't realise I was wearing any most of the time.

Celeste stepped into a long cotton skirt. 'Poor Wallace, they must find you so confusing.'

'Not poor Wallace!' I blinked twice against my mascara wand. 'At least they know I have a crush on them. I'm out here with no clue.'

'I didn't tell them you had a crush, exactly. I just said you liked them.'

I twisted the mascara back into its tube. 'Well, it's been more than a week and they haven't made a move.'

'Maybe they're waiting for you to make a move.'

'Or maybe they're not.' I sighed dramatically and lay back on the carpet, looking up at Celeste. Her face was upside down.

It was past eleven by the time we were dressed and made up. I pulled the collar of the turtleneck right up to my chin, only to feel it edge back down again. We stepped into the kitchen.

Wallace was eating toast off a Peter Rabbit plate. Their hair was still wet from the shower. They smiled when they saw us. 'Hello Celeste. Hello Eve.'

I could already feel my face getting warm.

'If you guys are ready, can we go?' Alex was sitting on the couch. She had a black tote bag in her lap, and Sophie's lilac Kånken next to her.

I swallowed my disappointment. I'd have to get Wallace alone at the strawberry farm.

Sophie was standing in the kitchen. She was distracted by something on her phone, but looked up when she heard Alex. 'I'm ready.'

Celeste sat in the passenger seat because she was the best at giving directions. Alex opened the back door on the pavement side, and I walked round to open the one on the road. We got into the car and both paused, the middle seat gaping between us.

Sophie gave Alex a shove. 'C'mon, I need to get in there too.'

Alex muttered something I couldn't catch as she shuffled into the middle, letting Sophie climb in next to her. Sophie got out her phone and started typing, then backspacing and typing again. Alex got out her phone too.

This made me want to check my phone, but I resisted. I watched Alex scroll through her Instagram feed, so fast I couldn't see any of the pictures. I wished that I could be sitting up front, next to Wallace, but as the only non-flatmate in the car, I knew I had to be in the back.

I didn't know Alex or Sophie particularly well: we were more friendly than friends. I couldn't see Alex and I getting much closer, but she and Wallace had been friends even longer than me and Celeste, so I had to be nice. The two of them had a matching tattoo of a cloud on their left shoulder blade. I had seen the tattoos only once, when we all went swimming at the beach. I'd been meaning to ask Wallace what they meant.

Last time I'd been in this car, it was just me and Wallace. I'd stayed late at the flat and said I would walk home, but

Wallace insisted on driving me. The rose incense Celeste had been burning clung to our clothes and hair, filling the car as soon as we shut the doors. We sang along quietly to songs off Wallace's phone, and when they dropped me off I imagined leaning over and kissing them goodbye. I thanked them for the ride and fumbled with my seatbelt. Wallace's hands were in their lap. They looked at me expectantly, but I couldn't tell if they were expecting me to kiss them or to get out. I got out. They drove away, and I immediately wished I'd done something. I looked up at the moon and prayed for the millionth time that Wallace would give me some sort of sign.

That was two weeks ago. Since then, a David Bowie air freshener had been hung on the rear-view mirror. It made the whole car smell like dishwashing liquid.

'What did you two get up to last night?' Wallace twisted their head to look out the rear window as they pulled out of the street and onto the main road.

'Just talking, mostly.' Celeste glanced at me.

'Did you watch a movie?'

'Nah. We were too busy talking.'

Wallace nodded.

I was sitting directly behind them. They were wearing shorts. The hair on their legs was long, but wispy and light from the sun. Their knee was bare and innocent.

Celeste plugged the aux cord into her phone. This was the other reason I wished I could be in the passenger seat. Every song I played in Wallace's company was a secret message aimed directly at Wallace. I'd been arranging my Mission Strawberry playlist for weeks.

Celeste rolled her window down. 'Strawberry fields, here we come!' She turned up the volume.

The hula girl on the dashboard swung her hips. Sophie kept

typing and Alex kept scrolling. I tried not to feel annoyed.

'We went strawberry picking in my dream last night,' Wallace said over the music. They began describing the dream in extreme detail.

I had often wondered if anyone had ever told Wallace that it was generally considered boring to tell other people your dreams. I didn't find them boring. I always paid close attention to Wallace's dreams, hoping they could tell me things about Wallace I wouldn't have figured out otherwise.

Wallace finished describing the dream just as the song ended.

'Wow, symbolic,' Celeste said.

We stopped at the petrol station first. The rest of us transferred Wallace money for the drive while they went in to pay.

Alex put down her phone as soon as Wallace was out of earshot. 'I'm really nervous about Wallace's driving.'

'Me too,' said Sophie and Celeste.

Maybe it was because I couldn't drive myself, but I hadn't noticed anything so terrible about the way Wallace drove. I thought Wallace was hot when they were driving. I liked watching their hands on the wheel.

'We just need to make sure they don't get too distracted.'

'Yeah, call them out if they're not looking at the road.'

Wallace came running out of the petrol station— clutching an armful of ice blocks to their chest. 'I got us all ice creams!'

Alex looked suspicious. 'You paid for them? With your money?'

'There was petrol money left over.'

Alex raised her eyebrows. 'Of course. Did you remember to get Sophie a dairy-free one?'

'She can have the Fruju.'

'It's okay, I'm not really hungry.' Sophie was looking at her phone again.

A part of me wanted to reach over and take it off her, just to see what she would do.

'Aw c'mon, someone has to eat it,' Wallace said.

Sophie sighed and took the Fruju.

Wallace handed out the rest of the ice creams. 'A Jelly Tip for you, Eve.' They smiled when they passed it to me: pleased but shy.

'My favourite!' I couldn't even recall telling Wallace I liked Jelly Tips. Their remembering excited me. I peeled back the wrapper and took a bite, realising as I did so that I was starving. Celeste and I hadn't had time to eat breakfast before we left.

Celeste unwrapped Wallace's Trumpet for them while they drove us back onto the road.

'Seatbelt, Wallace.' Alex stuffed her Paddle Pop wrapper into the cup holder.

'Whoops.' Wallace clicked their seatbelt into place. 'Mission Strawberry, let's go!'

I grinned. It was funny hearing my words in Wallace's mouth.

Celeste held out the Trumpet.

'Thanks, Celeste.'

I watched Wallace in the wing mirror as they took their first bite. They got chocolate on their chin, and made no move to wipe it off. I imagined licking the tip of my finger and wiping it off for them. I imagined the two of us holding eye contact. I imagined them blushing and looking down.

'Can we play a game?' Wallace asked, turning to look at everyone in the car.

'Watch the road, Wallace!' Alex sounded more irritated than worried.

Wallace quickly turned back.

We debated over which game to play, eventually agreeing on Fuck, Marry, Kill.

'Wait, but do you fuck the person you marry?' I asked. 'Or is it, like, a sexless marriage?'

'I reckon it's a sexless marriage,' said Celeste.

We drove onto the motorway and everyone rolled their windows up. I immediately missed the cool air—Celeste was right about the turtleneck being hot.

'All right, Wallace first,' said Alex. 'Um . . . Quentin Tarantino.'

'No, it's stupid doing a guy for Wallace, they'll just kill him.'

Wallace laughed.

'Yeah, but if we do two guys they'll be forced to fuck or marry one of them.'

'Do three guys!'

'Nooo,' Wallace protested, but we were all laughing now.

'Okay, okay, so Quentin Tarantino . . .'

'Timothée Chalamet!' said Celeste, and we all laughed harder.

Wallace had extreme difficulty understanding how any male could be seen as attractive, and they viewed Timothée Chalamet as the epitome of this phenomenon. Just a few days earlier, we'd sat at their kitchen table scrolling through his pictures—Wallace asking in an almost panicked voice, 'Why do so many girls like him? He looks like a Victorian ghost!'

'Who's number three?' Sophie asked.

'What about . . . that teacher from *Glee*?'

'Oh my god, Mr Schue, yes.'

'Mr Schue, Timothée Chalamet, Quentin Tarantino, go.'

Wallace moaned and put their head on the wheel.

'Wallace! The road!' Alex yelled.

Wallace sat bolt upright.

The car in the lane next to us surged forward so we were driving next to each other. Three young girls waved manically from the back seat, grinning at me with an intensity I recognised. My friends and I had played Sweet or Sour when we were little, too. I waved back and they all bounced in their seats, high-fiving each other.

'Celeste's turn,' Sophie said. 'That boy who works at the bookshop.'

'Ooooh,' the rest of us chorused.

'Sam Clayton.' Sam Clayton came to all the flat's parties, but none of us particularly liked him. He was always describing things he found boring as 'beige'.

'And Eve,' Wallace said.

Celeste turned and raised her eyebrows at me.

I grinned and raised an eyebrow back at her.

'I'll marry Bookshop Boy. Kill Sam Clayton. And I'll fuck Eve.'

'Thanks, Celeste,' I said, trying not to laugh.

'You're welcome.'

'Let's do Celeste again,' Wallace said.

'Kurt Cobain.'

'And Courtney Love.'

'And Eve,' Wallace repeated.

This time I did laugh.

Celeste was laughing too. 'I'd kill Courtney. Marry Kurt. And fuck Eve.'

'Okay, okay,' Wallace said. 'What about, um . . . Sofia Coppola, Elle Fanning and Eve?'

Alex sighed. 'We get it, Wallace, you're obsessed with Eve.'
Everyone stopped.

Wallace shot Alex a betrayed look. 'Alex!'

Alex shrugged. Celeste turned her head just enough for us to make eye contact. Her eyes screamed at me.

None of us spoke for the rest of the song. My mind was spinning. Wallace hadn't denied it.

'I need the toilet,' Wallace said. They sounded sensitive, one push away from a tantrum.

Celeste spoke carefully. 'There are some shops ten minutes ahead.'

I imagined Wallace getting out of the car and slamming the door. I imagined undoing my seatbelt and going after them. I imagined saying, 'Wallace!' I didn't know what I would say after that. I imagined kissing outside the toilets. My heart sped up. I counted my breaths.

Wallace pulled over outside a McDonald's.

'I need to go too,' Sophie said.

Celeste coughed loudly and Alex nudged Sophie with her elbow, but she was already getting out of the car and didn't notice. Frustration burned through me, but it was soon followed by relief. Did I really want to kiss Wallace outside a McDonald's toilet? I would make a move at the strawberry farm.

Alex, Sophie and Wallace all went to the bathroom.

Celeste spun round to look at me as soon as they were gone. 'Oh my god, Wallace must have said something to Alex.'

'That's a good sign, right?'

'Um, yeah, it's crush confirmed. They're on to you and me, though.'

'No shit. What do you think they'd do if they found out?'

'I don't know.'

We both paused. Celeste and I had always joked about how we'd have to stop hooking up if things worked out with me and Wallace, but I'd never considered the reality of it. The thought of never sleeping with Celeste again felt sadder and stranger than I had expected. She stared into the space next to me and chewed her lip. I tried to read her gaze but couldn't guess what she was feeling.

The others came back to the car. Sophie's hair was wet at the front, like she'd been splashing water on her face. She pushed it behind her ears.

'Can we swap seats, Sophie?' Alex asked. 'I've been in the middle for an hour.'

Sophie grimaced. 'I get carsick if I can't look out the window.'

I found this hard to believe, considering she'd been on her phone for half the trip. I waited for Alex to look at me instead, knowing I should offer to swap when she did. Alex hissed something in Sophie's ear, too quiet for me to catch. Sophie glanced at me. My stomach sank. Until then, I had told myself Alex's feelings towards me remained at a steady neutral, but it was suddenly obvious that wasn't the case. Sophie rolled her eyes and whispered something back. Alex sighed. Everyone clambered back into their seats. I kept my body as close to the window as possible.

'I want to play another game,' Wallace said. Their tone was stubborn and childish. I could feel it irritating everyone else in the car.

'I can't think of any more games,' said Alex, resting her head on Sophie's shoulder. Her hip pushed slightly into mine. 'How far to the strawberry farm?'

Celeste tapped on her phone's navigation app. 'Should be forty minutes. We just need to get over the hills.'

'What about Truth or Dare?' Wallace suggested.

I nudged the turtleneck's collar up to my chin. It was starting to itch.

'You can't do dares in a car,' said Sophie.

'Truth, then?'

'It's 1pm, Wallace, we're not playing Truth now.'

'What about Never Have I Ever?' said Celeste.

'Yes! Never Have I Ever!'

I smiled despite myself. Wallace's excitement was infectious. 'Isn't Never Have I Ever a drinking game?'

'We could eat bits of bread instead,' Alex said. 'I'm hungry.'

Sophie pulled the paper bag of focaccia out of her backpack. 'All right.'

'Okay, I've got one.' Alex paused, then dissolved into hysterics. She laughed so hard she stopped making any sound. 'Never have I ever—' Alex lost her breath. Her words came out in a rush: 'Shat my pants in an art gallery.'

Wallace reached back and aggressively tore a large hunk of bread from the loaf. 'Fuck you, Alex.'

Celeste, Sophie and I cracked up.

'What happened!' Celeste cried.

'I drank a lot of coffee, all right? The toilet was hard to find.' Wallace gripped the wheel so tight I could see the whites of all their knuckles. I imagined touching their hand and watching their fingers relax.

Wallace swallowed their bread. 'Okay, my turn. Never have I ever been in an open relationship.'

Our giggles subsided. Celeste took some bread, but she'd been open with her last boyfriend. Was I in some kind of open relationship with Celeste? I decided it was safer to leave it.

Sophie tore off a nibble of bread.

'Huh?' Alex was startled. 'Since when?'

'What did I miss?' Wallace whipped their head round. This time Alex didn't notice.

'Since last week.' Sophie's voice had gone stiff.

'And you're . . . cool with it?' Alex asked.

'I think so.'

The car swerved round a corner. I leaned the other way so I wouldn't press against Alex.

'Have you hooked up with anyone?'

'No, it's only been a week.'

'Has Logan?'

'I could never be with someone who was sleeping with someone else,' Wallace interrupted.

My body tensed. This shouldn't have come as a shock, but it did.

'What if they didn't tell you?' Alex asked, still staring at Sophie.

'That's even worse! I would never be with someone who keeps secrets like that.'

My armpits were getting sweaty. I looked at Celeste, but her head was turned so I could only see the back of it. I tried to guess what she was thinking. I had no idea. I looked down at the sheer drop off the hill and felt dizzy.

'Can we please do another question?' Sophie asked.

'Of course,' said Celeste.

The car was silent for a moment. A new song started playing and still no one said anything. Wallace jerked the car away from the edge of the road and I clung to the door handle.

Celeste coughed. 'Why don't you ask a question, Eve? You haven't done one yet.' She twisted to face me. Her look was urgent and encouraging.

I knew I should use this opportunity to get things going with Wallace, but I had no idea how. 'I haven't got one.'

Celeste widened her eyes. *Come on!*

I shrugged helplessly.

She sighed, giving me a final look. 'All right then. Never have I ever invited someone strawberry picking when what I really wanted was to ask them on a date.'

Her words cut sharp. Sophie and Alex stared wide-eyed at their knees. I looked at Wallace in the side mirror. Their cheeks were pink, and they were smiling in the same way they had when they gave me the Jelly Tip. A part of me wanted to smile too, but it was overwhelmed by a nauseous feeling.

I ripped off a small piece of bread. My forehead was damp with sweat. I wiggled the window switch, but it was jammed. 'Can someone open a window?'

Alex looked at me. 'Why don't you take off your turtleneck?'

My cheeks got hotter. 'I haven't got anything underneath.'

'Does someone have another question?' Sophie asked.

Alex smirked. 'Okay. Never have I ever thought about someone in this car while masturbating.'

Sophie snorted. My cheeks burned as I tore off another piece of bread. Alex raised an eyebrow at me. Wallace reached back and took some bread too. I stared at their outstretched hand. Goosebumps pricked up all over my body: I was too excited to breathe. This was actually happening. As soon as we got to the strawberry farm, I would pull Wallace aside.

We were over the hills now, driving down into smooth countryside. Relief poured through the car.

'Hey look, we're practically there.' Sophie pointed at a sign on the side of the road featuring a strawberry with skinny yellow legs and a straw hat. A speech bubble from the strawberry's smiling mouth told us to turn left in three hundred metres. We sped past it. I could see the corner up ahead.

'All right,' said Wallace. They turned to Celeste, then to everyone in the back seat. There was a sneaky look on their face. 'Never have I ever had sex with someone in this car.'

I went very still. I stared at Celeste's hands, willing them to stay in her lap. *Please*, I begged her. My stomach swarmed with guilt. *I'm sorry I'm making you lie, but please lie.* Alex glanced at my neck. I kept staring at Celeste's hands.

Celeste yelled 'Fuck!' before I realised what was happening. By the time I did realise, the car was already crashing. I remember the sound of Alex breathing in—so loud it seemed to suck all the oxygen out of the car. I remember the seatbelt cutting into my torso. I remember salt and crumbs and rosemary flying in the air. I remember the hula girl doing somersaults. I forced my head back into my seat. Everything spun. I couldn't tell if the car was shrieking or if it was one of us. Someone's nails were digging so hard into my thigh I was worried they'd draw blood. The car swung to a stop and we all flew forward, my face smashing into Wallace's headrest. I fell back into my seat. The salt and crumbs and rosemary collapsed from the air, showering over our heads. My whole body was shaking.

'Is anyone hurt? Is everyone okay?' Alex's voice sounded fuzzy and faraway.

My ears were ringing like I'd just left a concert. My hand trembled as I lifted it up to my nose. It felt crushed, but there was no blood.

Someone started crying. It took me a long moment to realise it was Wallace. I had never imagined them crying before. The sound scared me.

'I'm okay.' I could barely hear Celeste above the ringing.

'I think, I'm—' I sounded like I had a stutter. 'I'm okay.'

'I'm okay.' Sophie's voice was wobbly too.

I ran my hand through my hair, half-expecting it to come away wet with blood. Salt and crumbs fell into my lap. I realised then that Alex's hand was still gripping my thigh. I carefully touched her fingers.

'Oh!' She let go. Her nails left crimson crescents in my skin. They didn't bleed, but they stung like cuts. 'I'm so sorry, Eve!'

'It's okay.'

I started laughing. Alex started laughing too. Soon the whole car was full of laughter. We almost drowned out Wallace's crying, but not quite. The car smelled of something gassy and chemical. Our laughter was manic. None of us could stop shaking.

Eventually the laughing petered out.

'Do you think we should . . .' Celeste paused. 'Check on the people in the other car?'

I hadn't realised until now that there was another car. My heart was beating unnaturally fast.

'I'll go,' said Sophie. I heard her car door open. Celeste opened her door too. The two of them gingerly pulled themselves out. Celeste's legs collapsed under her. Her body fell to the ground.

'Celeste, are you okay?' Alex and I reached forward.

'I'm good, I'm good.' Celeste picked herself up, with some help from Sophie.

I watched them shuffle together towards a white van. There was a deep dent in its front, and cracks in the windscreen. Some of the fencing on the corner had been knocked down by the van's back end. Green paddocks surrounded us. I could see the strawberry farm just ahead: a wide, low building with

REAL FRUIT ICE CREAM printed above its open doors. We could walk from here.

Wallace had stopped crying. I listened to them breathe in and out, in and out, like a child. I needed to get out of the car. I clicked open my door and shifted my legs around, careful to test they still worked before standing up. My whole body felt unbelievably light. My head was pounding.

The air smelled of sun and grass. A car drove towards us. The driver slowed down to look at the crash. He mouthed 'Shit' as he drove away.

The front of Wallace's car was completely mangled. It looked like a giant had stomped on it. One of the side mirrors was dangling off, and it seemed miraculous that the windscreen hadn't been smashed too.

Celeste and Sophie were talking to a woman standing outside the van. She held a little boy on her hip, and a little girl was standing next to her, an ice-cream tub gripped firmly in her small hands. She kept jumping up and down. The little boy was dead silent and very still. They all seemed fine, but looking at the children made me feel sick. The woman looked at Sophie and Celeste with concern.

A man on a phone paced up and down the side of the road. I could hear him talking as I got closer. 'She clearly wasn't looking at the road. Fucking careless.'

I winced. Celeste reached out and held my hand.

The man hung up. 'Police and ambulance are on their way.' He put his phone in his pocket. 'I need to sit down.'

'Are you sure none of you girls are hurt?' The woman turned her concern to me.

'I'm okay,' I said.

The little girl grinned. The little boy stared blankly.

'I think we should all sit down,' the woman said. 'We're

all in shock. You girls sit, I'll go help your friends out. Ella, sit with Daddy?'

'I want to sit with the big girls,' said Ella.

'I'm sure the big girls want to talk about big girl things, love. You sit with Daddy and Toby.' The woman passed the little boy into the dad's arms. He still didn't make any sound.

'She can sit with us,' Sophie said.

Celeste and I nodded.

The woman gave us all a tight smile. The concern had been wiped from her face. She looked at the dad. 'Keep an eye on her?'

He nodded.

We all sat down on the gravel. Sophie let out a long breath.

Ella plonked the ice-cream tub in front of her. 'Daddy said the f-word.' Her expression was triumphant.

I watched the woman lean over to talk to Alex and Wallace, who were still sitting in the car. I couldn't see her face, but her arms were folded. I listened closely. She was hissing at them. I watched Alex's mouth repeat the words *We're so sorry, we're so sorry, we're so sorry.* Wallace wasn't saying anything. The woman shook her head and turned, giving me a brief glimpse of her face. Her expression was even more furious than the dad had been on the phone. She kept hissing, and Alex and Wallace slowly climbed out of the car. The woman straightened up. When she walked back to Toby and his dad, her face was composed again.

Alex and Wallace followed a few metres behind. I could barely recognise Wallace. In the bright sun their skin was so pale they looked like they could disappear. Their eyes were wide and glazed over.

The two of them reached us and sat down. Wallace avoided looking at Ella.

'We went strawberry picking.' Ella peeled the lid off the ice-cream tub. She stuffed her small hand in, and pulled out a squishy fistful of berries. 'I'll let you have some.'

There was a long pause before Celeste said, 'That's where we were going too.'

She picked a plump strawberry and bit into it. Her other hand was still intertwined with mine. Mission Strawberry felt like days ago. I took my phone out of my pocket and checked the time. It couldn't have been more than fifteen minutes since we had been playing Never Have I Ever. This felt impossible.

Ella was staring at me. Bright red juice dripped down her chin like fake blood. 'You hurt your neck,' she said. 'In the crash.'

I touched my hand to my neck, then remembered the love bites. I glanced at Wallace, but they were staring at the gravel as if they'd been hypnotised.

'Mama said Daddy did nothing wrong,' Ella told us, taking another handful of strawberries. 'She said it was completely not his fault.'

Alex and Sophie both took a strawberry. Celeste squeezed my hand and I squeezed back. I looked at Wallace. Wallace looked at the ground. I imagined saying something.

YOU ARE NOW ENTERING THE GROTTO OF THE PROPHETESS

There was only one exhibit in the gallery that the girls had any interest in. It was a giant head—a woman's head, about the size of a car—painted entirely white. Her features were classical, except for her eyes, which were made of convex mirrors.

The head was lying on its side, like it had just been chopped off. It was in the centre of the room, on a raised platform, with steps leading up to it. A grey panel told them it was called 'The Grotto of the Prophetess'. The girls didn't care about the head itself: they wanted to see what was inside.

They walked round it until they got to where the neck should be. Instead, there was an oval door—hanging wide open. Two pairs of legs dangled out of the doorway. They looked like they belonged to year sevens, judging from the black leggings and pink Converse. When the girls looked past the legs, they could see at least another three kids huddled inside. There was a long queue of people waiting for them to get out, so they could have their turn.

'When are the boys getting here?' said Genevieve.

Angelica checked her phone. 'They're only coming for the artist's talk. We've still got hours.'

Mary looked around. The rest of their class was scattered across the gallery, but none of them were paying any attention to the art. Even the girls who were in the queue for the grotto were reading texts off each other's phones.

Mary loved Genevieve and Angelica so much it scared her. Before they became friends, she had watched them every morning on the school bus. The two of them always sat in the four-seater, across from Angelica's sister and her best friend. Mary had known they must all live far out in the rich suburbs, to get such good seats every day. By the time the bus reached Mary's stop, there were never any seats left. For the twenty-minute ride, she stood in a crowd of navy wool and gripped a yellow metal pole for balance.

Mary had become friends with Genevieve and Angelica only because she wore a Radiohead T-shirt on mufti day. She had been so honoured when they came up to ask her about it. They had told her later it took them hours to work up the courage.

The girls locked themselves into toilet cubicles and pulled down their tights. The hairs on their legs were still short enough to be spiky: none of them had shaved for the past two weeks. They wouldn't shave for the next two weeks either; not until the night of the boys' school dance. According to Genevieve, not shaving for a month would leave their legs especially soft.

'I can see you, Angelica,' said Genevieve, who was in the toilet furthest to the left.

The gallery bathrooms were famous for their reflective floors. There was enough of a gap beneath the partitions that you could see almost half of the neighbouring cubicle's floor, and the bathroom lights were cast at such an angle that you could also see a blurry reflection of whoever was sitting on the toilet next to you. Mary was careful not to look down.

'You're wearing purple undies,' Genevieve added.

Angelica kicked her foot under the partition, knocking Genevieve's ankle with her black leather school shoe.

Genevieve yelped. 'That's gonna bruise.'

They all hit flush, then stepped out and washed their hands with the bubblegum-pink soap from the dispenser. Genevieve and Angelica dried their hands with paper towels while Mary held hers inside the dryer. It was too loud for them to speak over. Genevieve squeezed Palmer's cocoa butter into her palm, then offered the bottle to Angelica, who offered it to Mary. This was Genevieve's smell. She hated having dry skin.

Genevieve and Angelica leaned in close to the mirror and passed a tube of waxy, vanilla lip balm between them. They rubbed the balm on the tip of an index finger, then applied it carefully to their eyebrows—shaping the hairs into place. They were both making funny, concentrated faces: Genevieve's lips were pursed into a tight pout and Angelica's mouth was a little open, her tongue just poking out. Their eyes were wide—transfixed by their reflections. Mary was transfixed too. Everything Genevieve and Angelica did was magic.

Genevieve spun round. 'You sure you don't want some lip balm, VM?'

'VM' was short for Virgin Mary. Genevieve and Angelica were technically virgins too, but unlike them, Mary had never even kissed anyone. The nickname wasn't offensive. She liked it so much she wasn't sure she ever did want to kiss someone.

'I'm fine,' she said.

'At least have some of this,' said Angelica, digging a blue

pot of Vicks VapoRub out of her backpack. She twisted off the green lid and scooped out a fingerful of the white, fluorescent goo. She rubbed it on her lips, then passed the pot to Mary. 'It makes your lips plump up.'

Mary sniffed it. The menthol scent cleared her nostrils immediately. She dipped her finger in and applied a tiny dab of the gel to her lower lip. It tingled and fizzed. She rubbed her lips together until it was evenly spread.

Genevieve was carefully filling her pout with red lipstick, drawing a much sharper Cupid's bow than she actually had. Genevieve wore lipstick only when she was seeing boys, and only when there wasn't much chance of kissing them. She wouldn't wear lipstick to the dance.

Angelica tied her hair into a high ponytail. In summer Angelica's hair would be almost white from the sun and the lemon juice she squeezed into it. Right now it was tinged green from her regular swims at the pool. Angelica always smelled faintly of chlorine.

When Genevieve had finished her lipstick, she perched on the edge of the basin. She tore a page out of her art pad and rolled it up tight, so it looked like a very long cigarette. She held it to her mouth and pretended to suck on it, then blow smoke. Mary got out her phone and clicked into the camera. Genevieve grinned. There was a flick of lipstick on her teeth.

'Do I look ugly?' she asked.

Mary shook her head.

The bathroom door swung open. It was Miss Millan.

'Get out, you three.' She was looking at Genevieve. 'This trip isn't just for fun. You have an assignment to write.'

Miss Millan went to the toilet and the girls walked back out into the foyer. Mary and Genevieve sat down on a bench while Angelica bought a Coke from the vending machine by the gift shop. They all took turns sipping. Genevieve's lipstick rubbed off on the can—staining all their lips slightly red.

'We look like vampires,' said Angelica.

Genevieve dived her face into Angelica's neck—leaving a faint dash of red on her shirt collar. Angelica cried out in protest, while Genevieve turned towards Mary and bared her teeth. Mary ducked out of the way before Genevieve could get to her. Her heart raced like Genevieve was really going to bite.

The girls wandered back to 'The Grotto of the Prophetess'. The queue had disappeared: the only people in the room were a gallery assistant and a few older visitors staring at paintings.

'Sweet.' Angelica charged towards the giant head.

The gallery lights bounced off its mirrored eyes. They all stopped at the neck's open door. Everything inside was creamy white. The floor was lined with plush sheepskin, and the ceiling was thick with swirling paint stalactites. A cluster of ice-blue gems glowed on the wall. They climbed inside. Genevieve took hold of the crystal doorknob and pulled the door shut behind them. The door had a tiny oval window too, but instead of glass there was a thick slice of agate, impossible to see through.

Angelica lay down on a pile of white shag cushions. The smell of warm sheepskin filled the grotto. Genevieve sat herself in front of the Prophetess.

The Prophetess was a small girl with no nose or mouth. She had the same mirrored eyes as the head she lived inside, but she was closer to the size of a cat. She sat with her legs folded, like children at school. Her skin was made of white seashells and she had straight black hair. In her hands she held a crystal ball, the same blue as the jar of Vicks VapoRub.

Genevieve put her hand on the ball and pressed down. It pushed like a button.

'Tell me Prophetess, is anyone in love with me?' Genevieve spoke like she was joking, but Mary knew she wasn't.

There was a short pause, then the Prophetess answered, 'For sure.' She sounded older than the girls expected. Her accent was hard to pick.

Genevieve let out a theatrical sigh, then pushed the ball again. 'Is there a difference between being in love with someone, and loving them?'

Mary held her breath for the delay.

'Don't count on it.'

Angelica reached for the ball, but Genevieve elbowed her out of the way. She pressed the ball for the third time, her eyes locked on Mary. 'Will the VM kiss anyone before she turns eighteen?'

'That's up to you.'

Angelica slammed her hand down on the ball before Genevieve could stop her. 'Will I have sex before I turn eighteen?'

The Prophetess laughed. 'Forget it.'

'Ugh,' said Angelica. 'I hate this thing.'

'You can't fight the truth, Angelica,' teased Genevieve.

Angelica jumped on top of her and they wrestled in the white fluff. Mary held her body out of their way, tensed against the wall.

There were three light taps on the door. Angelica and Genevieve sat up as the gallery assistant opened it. She looked only a few years older than them. Her face relaxed a little as she took in the three girls.

'No messing around in here, okay?'

They all nodded. She gave them a hopeful smile, then closed the door again.

'No messing around, huh?' said Genevieve, sliding one hand up Angelica's leg and the other up Mary's.

Angelica whacked her. Mary's leg jolted away.

'I have an idea.' Genevieve unzipped her backpack and dug out her pencil case.

'No.' Mary knew what was coming.

Genevieve pulled out the glow-pen.

'Oh my god, Genevieve,' said Angelica.

'What? They'll never know.' Genevieve uncapped it and held up her hand, so the pen's tip was hovering only an inch from the wall. 'What should I write?'

'Shh!' Mary's eyes darted around the grotto—checking for a recording device. Maybe the Prophetess had ears hidden under her hair.

Angelica shook her head. 'This is like . . . art. You can't draw on it.'

Mary shuffled so her body would block the door if the gallery assistant opened it again. 'Please don't write our names.'

Genevieve grinned. Her hand darted forward. She wrote a 'V' and then an 'M', though the pen's ink didn't show up on the wall. Mary felt a rush of pleasure cut through her nerves.

'Write: *and her heavenly angels, G & A*,' said Angelica.

Genevieve laughed and obeyed. When she'd finished she turned on the tiny light at the end of the glow-pen and shone it at the wall. The writing was hazy and disjointed, but they could just read it.

Angelica took a pen out of Genevieve's pencil case and rolled up her left sleeve to draw an eye on her wrist. Angelica only ever drew eyes. She was very good at them.

Genevieve put her hands in Mary's hair and began dividing it into three sections. Mary felt the same rush as before. Angelica glanced up, then pulled her own hair out of its ponytail so Mary could do hers. They plaited in silence. Angelica drew a wobbly, left-handed eye on her right wrist.

The gallery assistant rapped her knuckles on the door and they all jumped.

'Time to come out now, girls.' She was trying to sound cool, but they could hear the fear in her voice even through the wall. 'Sorry to be annoying.'

Genevieve sighed. 'The boys will probably be here soon, anyway.' She whipped the hair tie off her wrist and twisted it round the end of Mary's plait. She gave it a little tug, then opened the door to climb out of the grotto. The gallery assistant had already retreated to the opposite side of the room, but she was watching them.

Angelica passed Mary her special blonde hair tie and Mary secured the plait. 'It's a bit messy. You can take it out if you want.'

'Messy is good.' Angelica climbed out.

'Hey, you didn't ask the Prophetess a question!' Genevieve leaned so her head and shoulders were inside the grotto.

Mary shrugged.

'Don't be dumb, you have to!' Angelica poked her head in too.

'I'm not asking in front of you.'

'Come on girls, it's time to give someone else a turn,' called the gallery assistant.

'One minute!' Genevieve pulled Angelica out. She winked at Mary, then shut the door.

It was very quiet in the grotto with no one else inside. Genevieve and Angelica's giggles were muffled and faraway.

The gems on the wall pulsed lazily from white to blue, then dark again. If Mary squinted, she could imagine they were glow worms, and this was her underwater cave. She could almost hear the water lapping.

Mary blinked. She stared into the blue ball. She could see her face reflected, but it was all shrunken, like an alien. She moved her head from side to side, watching it warp and bend, then covered her reflection with her hand. The ball was glass cold. She looked at the Prophetess's blank face. The questions that constantly buzzed around Mary's head went silent. She shuffled her body closer and leaned in. The Prophetess's skin was rough and bumpy against her lips, but it was warmer than she expected. When Mary pulled back from the Prophetess, there was a red kiss print where her mouth should have been.

THE HEART-SHAPED BED

Alice had wanted a heart-shaped bed since she was sixteen, which was when she had started wanting most of the things she wanted now. She had imagined she would meet some Lolita-loving, Sugar Daddy type who would be completely into the idea of a heart-shaped bed—and pay for it, too. Instead, she had ended up with a boyfriend who was five years older than her and did something with computers that she didn't fully understand. They'd moved in together a year ago and slept on an old mattress the entire time.

'I am not letting you turn our room into some nineties brothel.'

'It won't be a brothel! It's only a bed!'

'This is just another one of your Lana Del Rey fantasies. It will be like when we took acid. You won't even like it.'

'That was only because you were seeing cool things and I was stuck thinking about mould. It wasn't fair.'

'Can you seriously imagine a heart-shaped bed in this room?' Eric gestured at the tangled mess of technology on his side of the room and the mountain of floral clothing on Alice's. One of the curtains was torn down, and Bad Jelly had made a good start on the other. Two half-empty bowls of cereal sat on top of the computer monitor, and Alice's mirror was blurry with make-up smudges. She began to see his point about the brothel thing.

'I'll pay for it?'

'Damn right you'll pay for it. You're still not putting it in here, though.'

Bad Jelly slithered into the room—her black fur all wet from outside. She stopped when she got to Eric's backpack, turned her head, and stared at him. Her eyes were freakishly round, and an especially pale shade of yellow. She clawed the backpack in long, slow motions.

'Don't.'

Without looking away from Eric, Bad Jelly began peeing on the backpack.

'Fucking devil cat!' Eric jumped off the mattress and ran at her. Bad Jelly scampered out of the room.

Alice had bought her when she was eighteen and Bad Jelly was just a tiny scrap of black softness, all blue-eyed and mewling. Alice had imagined her growing into a witch's cat—twisting figure-8s round her ankles while she cast love spells and did tarot readings. She would be peaceful and mysterious, and so would Alice. By the time Bad Jelly was three months old, she had scratched up the wallpaper, destroyed the rug in the living room and brought in a rat almost as big as she was. She never pissed or shat on anything Alice owned, but she pissed and shat on just about everything else, including all of her flatmates' beds, and the stovetop.

She took particular vengeance on Eric. She'd even pissed directly on him. It had been New Year's Day and he was very hungover. He wanted Alice to get rid of her after that, but Alice told him she'd get rid of him before she got rid of Bad Jelly. She'd been kicked out of three flats before she met

Eric, and not once had she considered giving Bad Jelly up. Alice couldn't get kicked out of this flat, because she was the leaseholder. Her flatmates knew to keep Bad Jelly out of their rooms.

'One day I'm gonna kill that cat,' Eric said, taking his things one by one out of the backpack and checking them for cat piss. He never would. Eric was actually an extremely non-violent person. He wouldn't even play video games where you had to shoot people. Whenever Bad Jelly brought in rats or mice, he picked up the squirming body with a paper towel and carried it back outside.

Eric went into the laundry to soak his backpack and Alice slid his laptop across to her side of the mattress. The heart-shaped bed would cost a lot of money, but she had trouble processing the exact weight of the numbers she saw online. Any number between $1,000 and $5,000 meant the same thing to her: expensive. Her understanding became even more confused by how beautiful the bed looked. The headboard was made of pink velvet, and it was heart-shaped too. The bed came with two sets of heart-shaped sheets, a specially designed comforter and heart-shaped pillows. It was everything she had ever wanted.

She clicked 'Add to cart' and then 'Proceed to checkout', just to see what would happen. She entered her address. The shipping calculator gave her a number. She blinked at the screen. She clicked 'Proceed to payment' and entered her credit details. She wasn't actually going to do it. She clicked next and waited for the 'Review order' page to load. Once she'd seen that, she would exit out. A Visa logo popped up on the screen, and a little grey circle that said 'Processing'. Alice froze. The page finished loading. 'Order complete! You will receive an email confirming your purchase.' Her phone buzzed.

Eric walked back into the room. As soon as he saw her face, he stopped.

'You didn't.'

'Hee hee,' Alice said nervously.

'No fucking way, please tell me you're kidding.' Eric swivelled the laptop towards him and his eyes went as round as Bad Jelly's.

'I'll call my mum and get her to transfer me some money.'

'Some "counselling" money? How much therapy does she think you need?'

'I'll say that Bad Jelly needs surgery.'

'God, you scare me.'

Alice leaned across the laptop and kissed his ear. 'You love it.'

Eric looked at her. 'I don't think I do.'

She messed his hair up. It had grown out of its usual style months ago and was getting stringy. Every time she looked at it up close, she felt like she was having an allergic reaction.

'When are you getting a haircut?' she asked.

'Soon. You can stop bugging me about it.'

'No one else will,' she said. 'I've seen what your workmates look like.'

Eric shook her hand off. 'Stop trying to distract me from the bed. Can't you cancel the order?'

'I'll try.'

DHL said the bed would arrive on Friday, so Alice called in sick to the pharmacy that morning. Eric would be working from home and could answer the door, but she was too excited to wait until 5pm to see the bed. Every time she heard something like a truck driving up the street, she hurried to the window. Two delivery vans came in the morning, but they only had parcels for her neighbours.

When the DHL truck arrived, she ran out to meet it. The couriers carried the heart-shaped mattress in first. It was wrapped in plastic, and so big they could only just get it through the front door. They left it propped against the wall in the hallway, and went back to the truck. Alice pressed her ear up against the plastic and heard her pulse echo. She kissed the plastic and rushed back outside. The couriers were carrying a series of large and heavy boxes towards her flat. Alice gulped. She had failed to consider that the bed would come flat-packed.

Eric looked up from his computer as the delivery guys brought the boxes into their room and dumped them where the mattress used to be. Alice had moved it into the garage that morning, to be taken to the dump. The delivery men went back outside to bring in another box.

Alice could feel Eric staring at her. She knelt down and began ripping off the tape.

'Did you realise it was going to be flat-packed?'

'Yes.' She crunched the tape into a sticky ball. 'I was hoping you might like to put it together.'

Eric laughed. '*Like* to?'

She opened the box. It was full of wooden slats, all different lengths and shapes. Alice stared at them. 'Please?'

Eric sighed and leaned back in his computer chair. 'I'm supposed to be working.'

She rushed over and climbed into his lap. 'But you work so hard already!'

Alice didn't really know if this was true. He did spend a lot of time at his computer.

Eric shook his head so his nose brushed her cheek. 'This report is doing my head in. I'd honestly rather be putting your bed together.'

'Yay!' She kissed his forehead. His hair was oily, but she held herself back from commenting on it.

The delivery men walked into the room, saw them, dropped the box, and went back out.

Alice cleaned the kitchen while Eric built the bed, even though it wasn't her week on the chore roster and the kitchen was mostly clean already. Eric had specifically asked her to stay out while he was making the bed—'It will stress me out if you keep sticking your head in'—but every few minutes she had to fight the urge to go and check how it was coming along. She knew Eric secretly loved building things. The bed was like a tricky puzzle, and he loved tricky puzzles.

She'd met Eric when he was working in a phone store, and had been instantly struck by his careful skill in putting her broken phone back together. He had good hands. They were the most masculine hands she'd ever seen. Everything about Eric's appearance was masculine: he was tall and broad and looked like he could transform into a wolf at any moment. When Alice was around him, she felt more feminine than she did at any other time. Alice had been the one to ask him out, and the one to invite him back to her house. He looked even more masculine when he was in her room, surrounded by all her little things. When he took her clothes off, he barely seemed to notice the silks and scalloped lace she'd dressed herself in—he was so focused on her body. This was great for the first few months, but sex became boring once she knew his body and all the things that it did.

Bad Jelly sauntered into the kitchen, then started doing the funny, stiff-legged walk that she only ever did in front of Alice. She gave Alice a look. When Alice laughed, Bad Jelly went back to walking normally. This walk had been an inside joke between the two of them since Bad Jelly was a kitten. Alice had tried to do impersonations of the walk for Eric, but he didn't believe her. The few times she had tried to convince Bad Jelly to do the walk in front of Eric, she'd stared at Alice with eyes that clearly spelled 'N-O'.

Alice filled Bad Jelly's bowl with biscuits and got out the toasted sandwich maker. Eric couldn't tell her off for checking on the bed if she brought food.

The bed was nowhere near done. Alice was annoyed at herself for bringing him the cheese sandwiches. It took him an eternity to finish them and get back to building. She put his plate in the dishwasher and sat down on the couch. Bad Jelly trilled as she jumped up next to her. She snuggled into Alice, her face at the same level as the phone screen. They scrolled through Instagram together, then an online clothing store, then looked at vegan recipes—all of which were too complicated. Time passed even slower than it did when Alice was working at the pharmacy. It was 3:30 now, which was when she would usually take her last break—i.e., sitting in the backroom for fifteen minutes and looking at her phone. Alice slouched further into the couch. If she fell asleep, the bed would be ready in no time, but the anticipation had her too wired.

She logged into her old Tumblr account. This meant she was reaching peak boredom. Most of the accounts she followed had been deactivated, with the exception of a few Lana Del Rey fan pages, a handful of 'nymphet fashion' blogs, and various other accounts with some combination of 'baby', 'angel' and 'coquette' in the URL. There was less porn than there'd been when Alice was a teenager, but the bans still hadn't been entirely effective. A decent portion of the posts on Alice's own page had been replaced with a grey square telling her they contained 'sensitive content'. The photos that remained brought Alice more happiness than she'd expected. Her blog was a fairly even split of retro decor and girls in nature. Scrolling through her page went something like: black-and-white photo of girl on a lonely beach posing nude with a long, sheer piece of fabric; sixties hotel room; girl in river holding garland of flowers; fifties diner; girl climbing tree in her underwear; conversation pit. It made her body fizz with excitement. She especially liked the photos of girls who looked like her: honey-haired girls riding bareback across sweeping hills, each feeding their horse an apple. Half of the girls on Alice's Tumblr were holding fruit of some kind. She set a photo of a girl standing in a cherry orchard as her lock screen.

When Alice was younger, she'd spent all her time out in nature too—swimming in lakes, collecting acorns—but now there wasn't time for any of this. She and Eric lived in a suburb with two McDonald's and barely any grass. She'd tried suggesting to Eric that he drive them out to the equestrian centre for a horse trek one weekend, or even out to the bush reserve for a walk, but he'd been confused by both suggestions.

'Alice,' Eric called out. 'It's ready.'

The heart-shaped bed was so beautiful it made Alice beautiful. She put on a matching bra and undies and rolled around on the silky comforter. She felt like Jayne Mansfield in her pink palace.

'Take a photo of me.' Alice swiped her phone to camera mode and held it out for Eric.

Eric looked up from his computer and rolled his eyes. She looked too good for him to protest. She leaned back on her elbows and Eric tapped the shutter button. She pointed her toes like a pin-up model.

'There you go.' He passed her the phone.

She flicked through the photos. 'These angles are horrible. Take them again.' She passed it back to him.

'Can we do this another time?'

'The lighting's good now. Just a few more.'

Eric sighed. He stood up this time. She sat on her knees and crossed her arms at the wrist, so her boobs were pushed together. She stuck her bottom lip out a little. She could see Eric getting hard.

She raised an eyebrow at him. 'Enjoying yourself?'

'Not really.'

She shifted her legs apart like she was straddling an invisible body and crawled forward on her hands, like a cat. Bad Jelly gave her an intrigued look from the other side of the room. She pouted into the camera lens. Eric had a full boner now, pushing hopefully at the crotch of his jeans. She snickered.

'Thanks.' Eric spoke in a monotone.

She lay on her stomach, propped up on her elbows. 'I'm glad I don't have a penis.'

'Good for you.' Eric held out the phone. She took it. Eric went back to his computer.

She deleted the first ten photos immediately. 'Eric, I look disgusting. Why didn't you tell me to lift my chin up?'

'I'm not a photographer, for fuck's sake.'

'But it's so obvious! I have a double chin!'

Eric didn't turn from his computer. 'You look fine.'

'I don't want to look fine! Please can you take some more?'

'I'm trying to work.'

'I'll do something nice for you afterwards?'

'Like what, scratch my head for twenty seconds then get bored and stop?'

She reached her hand off the end of the bed. Her fingers could just reach his thigh. 'I was thinking something more along the lines of . . .'

Eric sighed again. He threw out his arm and she put the phone in his hand before he could change his mind.

'Thank you, thank you, thank you!'

She moved quickly from pose to pose. Eric occasionally lifted or lowered the phone. His eyebrows settled into a concerned frown as he tapped at the screen. It was hard not to laugh with his dick sticking out so ridiculously, but if she focused on the camera she could ignore it. She tightened her bra strap and Eric fiddled with the phone settings. She sucked her stomach in. The camera flash popped in her face.

'Flash is unflattering, Eric. Turn it off.'

'Okay, I'm done with this.'

'Wait, let's get some with Bad Jelly.' She scurried off the bed, scooped Bad Jelly into her arms and hopped back onto the comforter. Bad Jelly tried to squirm from her grip, but Alice locked her against her chest. 'Quick, take some before she escapes.'

'You look like you're trying to strangle her.'

'Just take the photos, Eric!'

Alice turned her head to the side and grinned. She did a little fake laugh. Bad Jelly made a hissing noise.

'That's it.' Eric threw the phone on the comforter.

'No, please take more!' Bad Jelly wriggled out of her arms and leapt off the bed.

'I've taken at least fifty photos. You'll like some of them.'

'But I wanted to do some lying down!'

'I'm sick of this.' Eric stalked out of the room.

Alice grabbed her dressing gown off the floor and wrapped it round her body. She followed him into the bathroom. 'I don't understand why it's such a big deal. It'll only take another two minutes.'

Eric turned on the shower and pushed the mixer all the way to the blue side. 'I'm not your slave. You can't just tell me what to do all the time.'

Alice opened her mouth, then found she didn't know what to say.

'I spent hours building that fucking bed. And I don't know how you think we're going to sleep on it.'

She didn't know what to say to that either. Eric had tried lying down on the bed, but his feet hung off the end no matter how he positioned himself.

Eric pulled off his T-shirt and jeans and dumped them on the floor. His dick was still hard, but it was tipped at an angle that meant it was going away. He stepped into the shower and shut his eyes under the water. Alice stared at his back. It prickled quickly into goosebumps. His shoulders were tensed against the cold, sticking up out of his back like they wanted to break into wings.

'I need my own space.' He spoke louder than he needed to. 'I don't want to live in your little heart-shaped fantasy.'

Alice folded her arms across her chest. 'It's not my fault I want things to look nice.' She sounded pathetic even to herself. 'I can't focus when everything looks so ugly.'

Eric snorted. 'Focus on what? Instagram?'

A sting whipped through Alice. Ever since she'd mentioned to Eric that her average Instagram screentime was two hours and forty minutes a day, Instagram had been a dangerous subject. She felt Bad Jelly's sleek body slither between her ankles.

'Instagram's more interesting than you are a lot of the time, Eric.'

'Sure. Great. At least I'm doing something with my life.'

Alice threw her arm into the shower and yanked the mixer to its hottest setting.

Eric reared back from the scathing water. 'Bitch!' His body pressed against the shower wall and his arm darted around the steaming jets, trying to reach the mixer. His dick was shrivelled, like a deflated balloon.

Alice turned and left the room. Bad Jelly scampered after her.

They got Burger King for dinner. Alice intentionally forgot to order Eric's onion rings, and after that she could mostly forgive him for the fight. Eric forgave her too, as he always did, but the problem of where they were going to sleep remained.

'Could you just, kind of, curl up?'

Eric shuffled his body into a fetal position—the pinkness of the bed adding to the womb-like effect. 'I think I'd be more comfortable on the floor.'

Alice threw herself down next to him. She could feel her hair fanned out on the comforter around her head, like a princess. She wished it was curly. 'You can't sleep on the floor. I'd feel too bad.'

Eric turned onto his back so he was facing the ceiling. She stared up at it too. The ceiling had always been her favourite thing about this room. It looked like icing on a wedding cake—all vines and roses and scalloped edges.

Alice reached her hand up to pat Eric's head, but drew her hand away when she felt the grease. She wiped her palm on his T-shirt.

—

Eric tried to bring the old mattress back in, but it wouldn't fit on the remaining floor space. At bedtime, he lay down a sleeping bag, with some sheets on top. He tucked himself up with their old duvet and pillows. Neither of them spoke about how long this was going to last.

Alice pulled the silky comforter right up to her chin. She was small enough that she could sleep right in the centre of the heart: her body forming a straight slice down its middle.

Bad Jelly leapt onto the bed and curled into her own heart shape. Alice could hear a soft, rumbling sound. She leaned her ear towards Bad Jelly.

'Eric! She's purring!'

'What?'

'Bad Jelly doesn't purr! I've never heard her purr before!'

Eric muttered just loud enough for her to hear. 'I'm sure this is what she's always wanted.'

Alice slept with her hand resting on the bridge of Bad Jelly's head. Eric's tossing and turning didn't disturb her once.

While Eric took the old mattress to the dump, Alice gave their bedroom the best clean it had ever had. Now that she had the heart-shaped bed, the rest of the room needed to live up to it. She hung up all her dresses and folded her skirts and tops. She hooked the curtains back onto the rail. They seemed uglier than they had before. She would have to buy new ones. Eric's desk seemed uglier too. The heart-shaped bed made his technology look out of place. Surely he didn't need all of it in here. She unplugged a few unnecessary-looking things and moved them out into the hallway. She pushed the rest of it far under the desk, hidden from sight.

When the room looked as good as it possibly could, Alice put on a sheer slip and stretched out on the bed with her laptop. Now that she had a heart-shaped bed, anything felt possible. All the purchases she'd held herself back from making in the past—on the grounds that they were too excessive, too expensive—now seemed like reasonable investments. First she searched 'red velvet curtains buy'. She compared prices, plus shipping, on different sites, and checked for promo codes. The store she ended up buying from also sold colour-changing light strips, and when she added those to her cart the shipping was free. She bought a pink vase in a shell shape and a white statue of Aphrodite. She bought a set of pastel-coloured storage crates. Adrenalin shot around inside her. She counted the order confirmations in her inbox. Fourteen.

The first thing Eric did when he got home was carry the stuff Alice had put in the hallway back into their room.

'What are you trying to do?' he asked. 'I need this.'

'You can't need *all* of this.' She waved her hand towards his desk.

'Yeah, I do.'

'But it looks so bad. It clutters the room up.'

'What about all your stuff?'

Alice had arranged her things as neatly as she could, but they still took up half the room. 'My things look nice.'

Eric cast his gaze around the floor. 'And where'd you put the sleeping bag?'

'Under the bed. I just rolled it all up.'

Eric shook his head and knelt beneath the desk to plug his things back in. Bad Jelly crept up behind Eric. She paused, then threw her body at his back—latching on with her claws.

'For fuck's sake!' He threw Bad Jelly off, sending her flying a good metre. She let out a savage growl that sounded more like a dog than a cat, and ran out of the room.

'Eric!'

He flashed her a look and shock hit her. There were tears in his eyes. She had never seen Eric cry before.

'You need to get rid of that cat.'

Alice didn't say anything.

'And you need to sell that bed.'

'You need to shut up,' Alice snapped.

Eric turned to stare at her. The tears were gone. 'You're a brat.'

Alice shrugged. 'Fine.'

Even Alice's dreams were beautiful when she slept in the heart-shaped bed. She dreamed she was a girl in a white dress running through a green field. A girl eating pomegranates on a red picnic blanket—thrown down in the middle of a meadow. A girl with daisy chains in her hair. A girl sitting in tall grass, holding a lamb, then a baby deer.

Alice woke up to Bad Jelly walking over her face. The firm pads of her paws pressed into Alice's forehead. Her fur smelled like straw. Alice pushed her off and sat up. The room was mostly dark, but she could see Eric sleeping on the floor. He'd still been sitting at his computer when she went to bed. They'd argued over whether to turn the light off. They'd both said 'Love you' before she fell asleep.

Alice climbed down from the bed so she was sitting next to Eric. He looked almost beautiful when he was sleeping. He could be a statue. She pushed his hair out of his face, and it flopped onto the pillow like a dead thing. It pained her to look at it. She turned towards her bedside table, and the marbled cup of stationery on top. The slim handles of her sewing scissors glinted in the dark. She reached for them.

She cut in long and satisfying snips, so soft that Eric didn't even stir. The severed locks of hair curled like ferns on the pillow.

RAT TRAP

I had entertained the idea of calling Lena about a fake rat for a long time before I actually did it. It all started at her kitchen table, the night before I moved into my new flat. It was close to midnight, and we were the only ones up. We were confessing our most irrational fears, and I had just told her how terrified I was of a rat getting into my bedroom. She laughed at me in a way that I liked. Then she said:

'If there's ever a rat in your room, call me and I'll come get it.'

Lena always said things like this: things that suggested we would be friends far into the future. We'd only known each other for a few months. The problem was that I wanted to be more than friends far into the future. Sometimes it seemed like she did too. There was undoubtedly some sort of tension between us. I felt it flickering whenever we held eye contact, like electricity. Other times it felt less like electricity and more like a giant rock—sitting between us, preventing our bodies from moving any closer. This all became harder to gauge when we were with our friends, which was most of the time. After I moved into my new flat and stopped spending so much time at hers, we almost never saw each other alone.

I invited her over to mine multiple times, but something always led her to cancel. After three weeks had passed and she still hadn't come over, lying about a rat felt like the only option. It helped that the flat was weatherboard, and we had a compost heap outside my window. Every time I threw my scraps in there I was convinced I could see a rat, but it always turned out to be a bird.

Lena picked up on the fifth ring. My heart was beating so hard I thought I would vomit it up.

'Hello June,' Lena said.

My mouth moved involuntarily into a smile, as it often did when I was around her. I felt my cheek getting hot against the phone screen.

'Lena, I'm experiencing a disaster.' I had planned that line, and exactly how I would say it: half-joking, half-scared.

'Oh no, are you okay?'

'Um, there's a rat in my room.'

'Oh no. Your worst nightmare.'

I couldn't help grinning. I hadn't expected her to remember. 'It really is.'

'How big is the rat?'

'Like . . . as big as a shoe.'

'That's big.'

'Maybe a small shoe, I don't know.'

'Okay . . . have you set up a trap or anything?'

'No, I've shut the door. I don't want to go in while it's there.' Actually I was standing right in the middle of my bedroom, pacing as we talked.

'Oh dear. Okay. I'm free in twenty minutes. I can come then?'

'Are you sure?'

'Yup, I'll be there in half an hour.'

'Thank you so much.'

Of course, I already knew that Lena finished work at 4pm on Tuesdays, and that she was usually free on Tuesday nights. I had thought about all of this in the past couple of weeks. I had showered, shaved and washed my hair two hours earlier, giving it sufficient time to dry. I had put perfume on earlier too, so it wouldn't smell too fresh by the time she arrived. I'd picked a cotton dress that looked casual enough to be something I would wear around the house, but also sexy. I'd curled my eyelashes, and applied the lightest lick of mascara.

Usually when someone I liked was coming over, I would put this amount of care into cleaning my bedroom too. But it would look suspicious if my room was too neat, after a visit from a rat. I tipped over my laundry basket and messed up the duvet a bit. I left the wardrobe slightly ajar. I also dumped a towel outside my bedroom, so it looked like I had tried to block the gap under the door after shutting the rat inside.

I checked my reflection in the mirror. My cheeks were still flushed from talking to Lena. The dress really was quite sexy—maybe it was too much? No, it looked good, and it was too late to decide on something else anyway. But should I wear socks? I took them off. They were clean, white cotton. I inspected my feet for blisters, or any other imperfections. They were fine. I looked in the mirror again. Socks were more casual—more homely—but bare feet added to the summery feel of the dress. I dumped my socks by the laundry basket, like they'd just fallen out.

I was lying on my bed willing my heart to stop beating so hard when Lena knocked on the door.

'Fuck, fuck, fuck,' I whispered, jumping up and checking my reflection again. My cheeks were still red, but that was good. I needed to look freshly startled.

'Hey!' I said, opening the door. Lena's face made me so nervous it was hard to look at her. 'You are not going to believe what just happened.'

'What?' She seemed calm. This made me more nervous.

'I opened my bedroom door and the rat just . . . ran right out, and then it ran into the kitchen and out the back door and now it's just gone!' I held the excited look on my face, waiting to see if she'd fall for it.

'Oh!' She did. 'That's good.' She laughed but looked slightly awkward. She still hadn't stepped through the front door.

'I was going to call you but I figured you were already driving. Do you want something to eat?'

'Oh. Um, okay.'

I knew Lena would never say no to free food. I'd seen her sneak second free samples at the supermarket, and when we'd been to an art opening together, she'd spent the whole night standing by the cheese.

She stepped inside and I shut the door behind her. I was still struggling to look at her face: we'd held eye contact for barely a second since she got here.

'What do you feel like? I've got chocolate, crackers, heaps of fruit . . .' This was only the beginning of the food I had bought. There were also frozen dumplings, ripe avocados, a fresh loaf of ciabatta, ice cream and a lot of fresh vegetables.

She laughed. 'I want all of those things.'

'I'll make us a platter.'

We walked into the kitchen. 'This is the kitchen,' I said, waving a hand around. 'And that's the living room.' I pointed through to where the couch and the TV were.

Lena kept her hands in her pockets and nodded. She was

wearing work pants that were stained faintly with grass and mud. 'Who are your flatmates?'

'Well, there's Katya, but she's at work most of the time. Her parents are the landlords.' I slid the ciabatta out of its paper bag onto the breadboard. 'Then there's Henry. He's cool. He cooks good food.'

I loved Henry, even though he was mostly silent. When we did talk it was always in the kitchen, always for at least an hour, and almost always about our love lives. I knew a lot about his Grindr dates, but not much else. He knew about every coffee Lena and I had drunk together, every afternoon we had spent sunbathing in her backyard, every late night chat, but he had never even seen a picture of her.

Lena peered out the back door. 'You have a garden?'

'Yeah, it's cute. Go look if you want.' I opened the fridge and got out tomatoes, gouda cheese and a punnet of hummus.

'I wonder if the rat's out there.'

I kept my face behind the fridge door. 'Ew, I hope not. It was so yuck.'

'Show me how big it was, with your hands?'

I looked at Lena to check she wasn't joking. She wasn't. I held my hands what I guessed to be a rat's length apart.

'Gosh, that is big. How do you think it got in?'

'Hopefully just through the door. I'm scared it could've come through the crack in the wall by the toilet. Or through the broken window in the laundry.'

'If there's one rat, there's definitely more.'

'Fingers crossed we're the exception.'

I needed to change the subject. All this lying was making me feel nauseous.

'What have you been up to?' I made an effort to hold eye contact as I asked the question. Lena's eyes were a pale grey-blue. She had a spot on her chin, but her face was even lovelier than I had remembered.

Lena stared back at me, then looked away as she started talking. 'Uni, mostly. I've been kind of stressed. Even work's getting busy, lots of cruise ships coming in.'

Lena worked in a wildlife sanctuary, cleaning and gardening. There was always a bit of dirt under her fingernails. 'We've been having rat problems too, actually.'

'Oh yeah?' I opened a packet of oat crackers and began arranging them in the corner of a large tray.

'Yeah, a little girl said she saw one running around and now everyone's freaking out that the takahē eggs will get eaten. She might have made it up, though.'

I kept my eyes glued to the tray. I placed the hummus and cheese on either side of the crackers, then glanced at the clock. It was only 4:30. I coughed. 'Do you want a drink? I have sour cherry gin.'

I knew Lena wouldn't like to turn down a free drink—especially something as exotic as sour cherry gin—but I also knew that she would never drink and drive. If she accepted, she would probably stay for at least a couple of hours to make sure she'd sobered up. Of course, I liked to imagine that after a drink or two we would end up making out and she would stay the night instead of driving home, but this was unlikely.

Lena grinned at me, almost as if she could read my mind. She shook her head, then said, 'Why not?'

I grinned back. This meant I could drink too, which meant I was more likely to make an attempt at showing Lena I liked her. I had no trouble telling boys when I liked them, but the thought of confessing anything to Lena made me feel like I was going to have a heart attack. The alcohol would at least calm some of my nerves.

I got out two glasses and poured in a small amount of the blood-coloured liquid. I topped the rest up with tonic and a squeeze of lemon, then passed a glass to Lena.

'Cheers.' I clinked mine against hers and we both took a sip. It was strong. Lena's eyes widened a little and I laughed, apologising.

She laughed too. 'You've got a heavy pour.'

We drank and talked. Lena sat at the kitchen table while I stood at the counter preparing the food. The platter looked like something from a catering event: it could have fed at least five people. I carried it to the table.

'So many things!' Lena gasped.

I cut a piece of cheese and put it on a cracker with a sun-dried tomato. Lena dipped a piece of bread in the hummus.

'I'm sorry I cancelled on you all those times,' she said, taking another sip from her glass. 'I've been in a bit of a hole, to be honest. But I think I'm back on track.'

'That's okay.' I smiled at her. It was sweet hearing her apologise, but I always forgave Lena within a day of her cancelling on me anyway. Sometimes I would be upset for an afternoon, but all it took was another message from her and I'd be back to dreaming.

Lena finished her drink and I offered her another. She accepted, nibbling on a piece of melon. I tried to pour less into our glasses this time, but the first drink had impaired my judgement and they ended up about the same.

We talked about uni and whether Lena should study postgrad or not. She had a major in geology and a minor in botany, which were both things I knew nothing about. I loved listening to Lena talk about these things, even when I didn't completely understand. I loved imagining Lena growing us a garden like something out of Beatrix Potter, in a distant future where I baked bread and infused citrus peels in vodka. I loved thinking of all the rocks and fossils Lena could find for us, to line up on our shelves and windowsill.

'I'm worried it will be too much pressure,' Lena said. 'I don't want to procrastinate a ten-thousand-dollar degree.'

A part of me didn't want Lena to study postgrad either, because then she'd be even busier than she was already. That said, if she was enrolled there'd be no chance of her moving cities any time soon.

'You love it though, right?'

Lena nodded.

'You should do it then.'

Before I knew it, we'd both finished our second drink and Lena was laughing at me as I tried to pour the tiniest possible amount of gin into our glasses. She seemed in no rush to leave. This was good: I wanted to keep her here as long as possible.

'Hey, I haven't even seen your room,' she said.

I thought I could hear suggestion in her voice, but maybe I was making it up. 'Shall we?'

Lena nodded. 'We should check for holes in your walls. Maybe we can find where the rat came in.'

'Yeah, for sure.' I handed her a refilled glass as she stood up from her seat. 'Whoa,' she said, catching her balance.

We hurried, giggling, out of the kitchen. I walked right into the couch. 'Whoa!' Our giggling turned into cackling.

I kicked the towel out of my doorway. 'Here we are!' I sat down on the edge of my bed. There weren't any chairs, so aside from the floor it was the only place to sit.

Lena stood in the middle of the room, turning in slow circles. 'Oh, you found a good one! It even has a stand-in closet!'

When Lena was helping me search for a room, she'd called every closet that was big enough to stand in a 'walk-in closet'. I had mentioned that my dream bedroom would have one, and Lena was excited to find so many potentials. Eventually I had to explain to her that a walk-in closet is like its own little room, much bigger than any of the closets in the rooms we were looking at. 'That's not a walk-in closet; it's a stand-in closet,' I told her. 'Stand-in closet' quickly became a part of our shared vocabulary. 'Two people could stand in there,' she would say, pointing at a photo on 'Flatmates Wanted'.

Lena grinned at me. 'Wow, four people could stand in this one. Maybe even five.'

'Shall we stand in it?' I spoke with enough humour in my voice that Lena could laugh it off if she wanted, but not so much that she had to.

'Okay.' She had that troublemaking look she often got when she was drunk.

I jumped up and opened the wardrobe door.

'You first,' said Lena.

'What a gentleman,' I teased, pushing a bunch of coathangers to the side and stepping into the space left behind. Lena stepped in after me. Both of us still had our drinks in our hands. I pulled the door towards us, so only a crack of light shone in. The door had no handle on the inside, so I had to pull on the door itself, and slither my fingers back inside through the gap. The closet smelled of dusty linen and laundry powder.

Lena slid down the back wall until she was sitting. I slid down after her.

'Wow, it's been a long time since I was last in a closet,' she said.

'Tell your grandparents that.'

We laughed loud. I could feel Lena's breath warm on my cheek. We sipped our drinks.

'Did I tell you about my grandma trying to set me up with my cousin? The Jehovah's Witness?'

While Lena was telling the story, I slipped my fingers into the narrow gap between the bottom of the door and the carpet. I swung the door ever so gently back and forth, letting in a tiny breath of light every time I pushed out. I pulled it in further than before. There was a satisfied click.

Lena stopped mid-sentence. 'What was that?'

It was suddenly so dark in the closet that I couldn't see her face.

I dragged my fingers out from under the door. It hurt more than I expected. I pushed on the door. It didn't open.

'Um—'

'We're not stuck in here, are we?'

'Ha ha . . .'

'June!' Lena sounded shocked, but also amused.

'There must be some way we can open it.'

I put down my drink and shuffled onto my knees. I pushed hard against the door, both palms flat. It didn't budge. I squeezed my fingers underneath and tried to wiggle it, but that didn't work either. Lena got up and pushed too. My eyes had adjusted enough to see her now.

'Damn, it's really stuck.'

We sat back against the wall.

'Do you have your phone?'

Lena checked her pocket. 'It's in my bag.'

'I left mine in the kitchen.'

'Shit. Should we shout?'

'None of my flatmates are home.'

'Far out. We're really trapped!'

We were silent for a moment, then both cracked up. I had never heard Lena laugh so hard before. Our bodies fell into one another—my mouth brushing against Lena's cottoned shoulder. Electricity fizzled through me. Our giggles gently subsided. We coughed. I searched the dark for my drink, hovering my hand until it touched on cool glass. The tonic had lost its fizz. I gulped down what was left, and heard Lena do the same.

'Well,' Lena's voice had lowered. 'If we're stuck in here . . .'

I could only just make out her eyes. She blinked. We both leaned in, still hesitating even in our drunken state. As soon as our lips touched, I felt a confession bubbling to the surface. We kissed and I fought it down. I was terrible at keeping secrets when I was drunk; I should have considered this. I moved my tongue into Lena's mouth, hoping she would bite it for me. The taste of sour cherry gin dissolved. Her mouth was sweet. Lena's fingers touched my arms. I was running out of breath. She pulled softly back and I caught it again.

'I lied about the rat.' The words blurted out before I could stop them. I froze, unsure of whether I wished I could take them back.

Lena grinned. Her teeth glowed white in the dark. 'I thought so.'

It took me a moment to be able to speak. 'What?'

'Well, I believed you when I was driving here. But when there wasn't a rat, and you made all this lovely food . . .'

I covered my face with my hands. I was embarrassed that she'd figured it out, but more embarrassed by how convinced I'd been that she was fooled.

'Was trapping us in the closet part of your plan too?'

I could hear her smiling. 'No, this part hadn't crossed my mind.'

She moved her hands down my forearms until our fingers interlocked. She took a deep breath. 'I lied about something too.'

The closet felt hotter than it had before. 'Really?'

'Yeah. It's not fun like yours, though.'

Did she have cancer? A girlfriend? 'That's okay.'

Lena ran her tongue over her top lip. 'I lost my job.'

'Oh!' I never would have guessed that. 'When?'

'Nearly a month ago. They couldn't renew my contract.'

I nodded, slowly. Lena had cancelled on me at least twice in the past month with work-related excuses.

'I've found a new job now. I'm starting at the gardens next week. I'm completely broke, though. I've been living on rice.'

I squeezed Lena's hands. 'You should've told me. I would've cooked for you.' I would've cooked for her every night, if it meant spending time with her.

'Exactly,' she said. 'And then I would have felt like a charity case. It's embarrassing enough with my flatmates, let alone you.'

'But I would've been so happy to! I love sharing things.'

'I know. I just wanted to come round to your new place when I could bring something with me. Dessert or whatever.' I saw the white of her teeth as she smiled again. 'And then you tricked me with the rat and I got sucked into eating here anyway.'

I forced a smile too.

She pulled my hands into her lap. 'I'm sorry I lied to you. I haven't been leaving the house much. I've been pretty low.'

'I could've cheered you up.'

Lena laughed. She kissed me again. Her hands wrapped round my neck. I moved my hand from her waist down to her bum, but the thick, coarse fabric of her pants meant I couldn't feel much. She ran her fingers across my collarbone and my skin pricked up. I could feel the dresses in the closet tickling my bare leg. It almost felt like an animal.

I sat bolt upright. 'Holy fuck.'

'What?' Lena was startled.

'I think I just . . .' I felt it again. This time, I yelped. I jerked my leg and something like claws scattered over my ankle. I jumped to my feet.

'Lena, I'm not kidding, there's a fucking rat in here. Or a mouse or something.'

'What?'

It ran over my feet and onto Lena's shoes. The volume of her shout shocked me.

'Fuck!' She kicked it upwards, landing the animal on top of my feet. I hopped, trying to throw it off. My foot landed on its body and I screeched. It was way too big to be a mouse. The rat squirmed out from underneath me. Sharp little needles bit into my skin.

'Help!' I screamed, banging on the door.

Lena gripped my arm tight enough to bruise.

I kept calling.

'Wait,' she hissed.

I stopped.

'Where's it gone?'

We stood statue-still, listening. There was an aggressive ringing in my ears, but the closet was silent. We waited for a scuttle, a scratching.

'Maybe it went back into the wall,' I whispered.

I saw Lena nod. Her eyes were wide and shining, even in

the dark. 'What time do your flatmates usually get home?'

'It depends.'

I listened to Lena breathe in, and then out. 'I really need to pee.'

'Oh.'

Neither of us said anything. She could pee in our empty glasses, if worse came to worst. The smell wouldn't be ideal, but so long as the rat stayed out of the way we should be able to manage it. Would Katya kick me out of the flat if she found us like this?

Something shuffled. I felt my chest clench, and then the rat shot across my toes and onto Lena. She cried out, accidentally kicking the door. I could feel the rat flailing all over the place—flinging itself over our feet and darting around our ankles. We shrieked and pounded hard against the wood. Our screams were even louder in the tiny space, drilling into my eardrums. The rat was shrieking too: horrible, high-pitched, squealing noises.

The door opened slowly and we shoved it, tearing into the light of my bedroom. I saw Henry's face in a brief flash of confusion and alarm. The rat leapt after us.

'Holy shit!' Henry darted out of the rat's way.

I jumped onto the bed and hugged my knees to my chest, my entire body shaking.

Lena looked manically around the room, then picked up my rubbish bin and tipped the contents on the ground. The rat dodged the rubbish and leapt over the socks I'd left next to the laundry basket. It zipped towards the bed, but there was no room under the solid base for it to squeeze through. It thrashed around, looking for an escape. Lena ran towards it and slammed the rubbish bin over its body. She crouched down, pushing the bin hard into the carpet. She was shaking too. 'Get a piece of cardboard,' she ordered Henry.

He nodded and ran out of the room. He came back with an unfolded pizza box and handed it to Lena.

'Thanks.' She tore the box in two and slid half under the metal bin. She carefully lifted both into the air, holding a flat hand under the cardboard so the rat couldn't escape.

I was impressed.

'Open the door for me.' She was already rushing out of the room—gripping the bin like it was a bomb that could explode at any moment. Henry ran ahead of her and opened the front door. I heard Lena run outside and free the rat.

Henry came back into the room first. 'So, what the fuck?'

I nodded, still unable to speak.

'I could hear your screams from down the drive. I thought you were being murdered.'

Lena stepped back into the doorway. 'Where's the bathroom? I'm busting.'

Henry looked at her carefully. 'Are you Lena?'

'Yes?' She seemed unsure.

He nodded, holding back a smile. 'Second door to the left.'

Lena rushed away.

Henry turned back to me, smiling now. 'You're lucky I came home before Katya.'

'I know.'

'She's gonna flip when she hears we have rats.'

Henry went to get a beer.

I barely moved from my curled-up position while Lena was in the bathroom.

When she came back, she walked over to the closet and leaned over, heaving aside a box I hadn't opened since moving in. She inspected the walls. 'Here we are.' She pushed back my dresses and nudged the box further to the left, revealing a section of the skirting board that had begun rotting away. She flopped down next to me on the bed. 'Are you all right?'

I lifted my hand. It was shaking like I'd just drunk a plunger of coffee. 'A bit spooked.'

She took my hand in hers. 'Fair enough.'

'I keep thinking I can still feel rats running over my feet.'

'God yeah, it was freaky enough with shoes.' Lena looked at my bare feet. 'Is that a bite?' She pointed at two small puncture marks near my left heel.

'I did feel something like teeth.'

'You need to wash this. You could get rat bite fever.'

I stared at her. 'Is this a trick?'

'No, I'm serious. It's real. Have you had tetanus shots?'

'I think so?'

'That's good. Let's go to the bathroom.'

Lena sat me down on the toilet set and found a facecloth and a bar of soap. She ran the cloth under warm water, then crouched on the ground and dabbed at the bite. I felt like a child—I hadn't been so taken care of in years. She rubbed the soap in small circles, then patted with the cloth.

'Do you have antiseptic cream?'

'Check the second drawer.'

The second drawer was Katya's drawer. She had strict rules about not taking anything from it, but Henry and I were always borrowing sunblock and cotton buds. Lena rifled through the creams and lotions until she found a blue and white tube. She applied the ointment gently. It tickled. I had to hold my foot back from kicking her.

'Okay, that should be good.'

She twisted the lid onto the ointment and I stood up from the toilet. Lena stood up too. Her face drained of colour.

'Are you okay?'

Lena lifted the toilet seat just fast enough. She crouched down and vomited into the bowl. The vomit was pink and faintly cherry-scented.

I hovered over Lena, holding back her hair. Usually I liked holding my friends' hair back while they were vomiting: it made me feel part of some great feminine tradition. But any pleasure I might have taken was overwhelmed by guilt. Had I given Lena rat bite fever? Food poisoning? Alcohol poisoning? Was she drunker than I realised? Should I have kissed her? I reimagined this whole afternoon with me as a man instead of a girl. It was like a low-budget thriller movie.

Lena pulled back from the toilet and hit flush.

'Phew, I feel better now.' She smiled up at me. She was so pretty, even with her eyes all bloodshot from vomiting.

'I'll bring you some water.'

I rushed out to the kitchen. Henry was reading a cookbook at the table, but he looked up when I came in. He drank from his can of craft beer and watched me fill a glass. When I got back to the bathroom, Lena was already rinsing her mouth out in the sink.

'Do you have any mouthwash?'

I gave her the water and took Katya's Listerine out of the cupboard. I'd buy her some more when it ran out.

'Thanks.' Lena gargled, swished and spat multiple times.

'I can get you an Uber home?'

'Nah, I'm okay.' She put the Listerine back and drank the water.

I paused. 'Do you want to lie down?' I felt slightly sinister asking this question, though I really did want to offer her a place to rest. Of course, a tiny part of me hoped she would magically feel great and we would end kissing on my bed, but I was expecting something more along the lines of her falling asleep and me cleaning up the kitchen.

'That would be nice.'

We lay on my bed. The curtains were open, and it was starting to get dark outside.

Lena turned on the pillow so she was facing me. I turned too.

'I'm so, so sorry.'

She laughed. Her breath smelled intensely of spearmint. 'It's okay. It's funny.'

'I promise I'll make it up to you somehow. I'll buy you the best present you've ever had.'

'You don't need to do that.'

'Do you think I'm a psycho?'

Lena laughed again. 'A bit. But I also kind of feel like we have to get married or something. This would be the craziest wedding story anyone's ever heard.'

I laughed too. I hoped she was serious.

GIRLS IN THE TUNNEL

The school bell rings and a deep blue sea of wool uniforms flows down the hill. White blouses poke out and in like sea foam.

The Hataitai girls trickle off. They file into the tunnel.

The younger girls tell it like myth. One of them wonders aloud why cars always toot in this tunnel, and another answers, *The ghost, duh.* She switches her sports bag to her left shoulder and explains that back when the tunnel was being built, some girl was murdered and buried in the fill. Now, people toot to keep her ghost away. On cue, a driver blasts their horn. A din of cars honk back. The girls cover their ears, but it doesn't make a difference. The sound is so loud it hurts. They're relieved when it peters out.

They walk side by side until a bike bell dings at them, and they scramble to let the cyclist pass. Their bodies press up against the cold concrete wall. A whip of wind sends hair into their faces.

The girls in the year above know the juiciest parts of the story. They yell it out to each other over the tooting. *She hooked up with a guy who was twenty-nine when she was only sixteen!* (An older sister recently told them about the half-your-age-plus-seven rule.) *His wife was dead, and he had six kids in an orphanage! He got the tunnel girl pregnant at seventeen!*

The girls all shudder. None of them want to get pregnant at seventeen, or eighteen, or nineteen. Past that, they're not sure.

The leader of the group turns and walks backwards, so she's facing her friends. *He worked at the building site for this tunnel. He was spotted digging here at night. Then the girl went missing.*

Someone screams, followed by a chorus of *Shh* and *Stop!* The scream echoes.

They stopped all work on the tunnel until her body was found. She was buried alive.

The senior girls have seen her photo. She looks sad. She sits on a garden chair with flowers growing at her feet, and stockings sag round her ankles. Her face is blurred.

The first girl breathes in deep as she enters the tunnel. She loves its petrol smell.

Her friends breathe shallow and only through their mouths. They're sure they can taste it. They'll spit on the ground when they're out.

One of the pedestrian lights flickers as they approach. It turns on, off, on, off, like it's speaking in morse code.

They all turn to look at each other. *The ghost!*

Her name was Phyllis Symons, one girl says. She did a presentation on the murder for history last term and has all the facts memorised. *Phyllis met George Errol Coats in 1930. By 1931, she'd had a fight with her parents and moved in with George.*

They lived in a boarding house, on Adelaide Road, her friend adds. *Across from where my dad used to live.*

Right. So soon enough, George got Phyllis pregnant. And just after that, he lost his job at the Mount Victoria Tunnel building site.

The girls argue over whether he'd worked on the tunnel itself, or at the neighbouring earthworks where the fill was dumped. One girl swears on her life it was the latter.

Phyllis went missing. George told their landlady she'd gone back to her parents, but he told someone else she was staying at her brother's house. He was arrested. More than a hundred guys were brought in to dig up the fill.

She pauses and looks round at her friends. Their eyes are wide.

Heaps of people came to watch. There was a crowd of six hundred by the time the pathologist arrived.

One of the girls asks what a pathologist is.

They figure out how people died, her friend explains.

Phyllis was found with her head wrapped in a scarf. The pathologist reckoned she was forced to kneel, then hit over the head with a spade and tipped into the hole. She tried to get up and was hit again. Her body was hunched up, so she must have tried to escape but suffocated in the soil.

The girls swallow hard. They feel the petrol fumes dark and gross in their throats.

In court, George claimed Phyllis jumped to her death, and he buried her in a panic—scared that he would get the blame. He admitted to hitting her once before, but said he only did it because she asked him to. There was evidence of an attempt to abort the baby.

A car horn blares extra loud and they all jump.

George got death for murder, though he never stopped saying Phyllis had killed herself.

The seventeen-year-old girls like to think the tooting began in honour of Phyllis, rather than to scare off her ghost. They enter the tunnel arm in arm, as if they're headed to the Emerald City. They wonder what she was like.

Apparently she was really quiet.

Teachers said she was backward at school.

They called her a simple girl.

Like you, hey? They elbow each other and laugh.

How does a sixteen-year-old even meet a guy who's twenty-nine?

He was working at a building site near her parents' house in Aro Valley. She brought him a cup of tea.

A woman with a pram walks towards the girls. They part ways to let her through and she thanks them. Her baby is asleep.

I always think about the letter she left under her mattress.

I always think about the shovel. George asked his workmate to leave it out for him. He said he had to bury a dog.

The girls' school ties feel tight round their necks. They pull at the knots but they won't loosen. They're thinking: *Phyllis was our age when she died.*

The oldest girls have read the newspaper clippings and asked their grandparents. They know Phyllis's name is spelled wrong on the tunnel's Wikipedia page. They know she's buried in an unmarked grave.

Two of the girls leave school during study period. One is carrying a purple box of fund-raising chocolate—half-full with paper IOUs. The other is eating a bar of Caramello. They wave at their friend as she drives past, and she toots back.

The girls don't notice the honking in the tunnel anymore,

and they're used to its petrol smell. They agree that once high school is over, they're never walking through here again.

I keep having this nightmare, the girl with the Caramello says. She runs her finger along the tunnel's concrete wall. *It's evening, and I'm the only one walking in here. There aren't any cyclists either. A whole lot of cars start honking, and I look up to see why. The tunnel's exit has closed in on itself. I turn around and it's the same behind me. There's no escape.*

The girls' phones buzz in their pockets, but they both ignore it.

Each end of the tunnel starts rolling closer, destroying all the cars in its way. Everyone's beeping and screaming. I wake up just before I'm crushed.

Walking through the tunnel always takes longer than the girls expect. They sigh a breath of relief as they step into the afternoon light. They pause to pull up their tights. When they get to the Four Square, they'll buy ice blocks and a dollar mix.

FRUIT

I went to the market every Sunday that summer, but I never bought any vegetables. I bought only the most exotic fruits: pomegranates, persimmons, a blood orange. I cut the pomegranate and the blood orange in half, then positioned them on a sunny patch of grass. I took photos and posted the best ones on Instagram. When I cut open a grapefruit and it was red instead of orange, I took photos of that too. I didn't particularly like the taste of any of these fruits, but I loved how they looked. I loved the ritual of picking apart a pomegranate and popping the seeds into my mouth. I loved the texture of citrus flesh on my tongue. I loved licking at the juice.

When I bought a punnet of raspberries, I stuck them on my fingers and ate them one by one, like in *Amélie*. I cut up strawberries and placed them on a china plate, sprinkled with icing sugar. I ate passionfruits with a tiny spoon. I bought a coconut and threw it at the concrete, over and over until it cracked, spilling milk on the grey-black. I ate blackberries in an old white T-shirt and let the dark juice drip all over it. I hung the stained shirt on the washing line and took photos of it flapping in the sun. I bought so many furry little peaches and apricots, so many shiny plums. I kept them in a basket in my room until they reached the perfect ripeness. When one was ready, I would take it into the shower and eat it while the water pummelled over my head. The girl I was in love with had told me to do this, back in autumn. We saw each other at least once a week through spring, but she ghosted me in summer.

I'd met Ada in July. It was the brightest full moon of the year and my friend Grace threw a party at her flat. There were a lot of linen dresses and designer hoodies. The lamp in the corner cast a mysterious glow over all of us.

Grace hugged me when I stepped into the room—followed by some other friends. We kissed cheeks and offered each other sips of our drinks. Conversations split off.

A dark-haired girl appeared in front of me. She was slightly shorter than I was, and wore a blue shirt tucked into white pants.

'What a lovely dress!' Her hand hovered down my sheer sleeve. 'You look like a goddess.'

Grace had mentioned Ada before, but I'd never known what she looked like. When I'd scrolled through her Instagram it was all trees and flowers: no photos of her. I was shocked by how pretty she was. Her eyes were sharp green and curious, with heavy eyelids. 'Bedroom eyes,' Grace called them later, though what struck me about Ada was how awake she seemed, how alert. She made everyone else seem half-asleep in comparison.

We sat together in the lamp's spotlight for the rest of the night. Ada asked a lot of questions. I wasn't used to this. Usually I was the one doing the asking. With Ada, it was hard to get a question in at all. This only intensified my curiosity.

She turned the lamp dimmer up and down while we talked, never taking her eyes off mine. I tried to imagine how I must look to her in all that changing light. Even mid-laugh, I was conscious of how I held my face.

We talked about me being an extrovert and Ada being an introvert.

'I like being around other people, but I don't need it,' she said. 'I'm happy on my own.'

Every time someone waved at me or came over to say hello, she would laugh and shake her head.

'Lemon Glow' came on and Ada tapped her fingers to the beat. We discussed birth charts, and Ada pulled up an app on her phone to see our compatibility. 'All ticks except for love and pleasure.' She smiled a small and sly smile.

Before Ada went home, she went through her backpack to check she had her wallet and keys. She pulled out a net bag of tangerines, with a hole already torn in the netting. She held one towards me. 'See you soon.'

I saved the tangerine for a whole week, lying on my bed and passing it from hand to hand while Grace and I talked about Ada on the phone.

'She's one of those people it's hard not to fall in love with, if she pays you any attention,' Grace agreed. 'I've never seen her look at anyone the way she was looking at you, though.'

'I think we're seeing each other this weekend.'

'Fun! Maybe you'll kiss.'

We didn't, but I was happy just to see Ada again. We made plans to go to a gig together later in the month. When I got home, I let myself eat the tangerine.

Some of the fruits I bought at the market I hadn't heard of before, like custard apples. Their name had me imagining a

78

creamy, vanilla flavour, with notes of cinnamon and apple pie. When I finally managed to tear open the thick skin and bite into the flesh, I spat it straight back out. The texture was grainy and the flavour was dull—not like vanilla at all. It was the same with lemonades. I expected a sugary taste of lemon-honey, but they were more like a too-sour orange.

Ada loved citrus fruits. 'I wish I could get all the nutrients I need from an orange,' she had said that August, digging her nails into the skin like she was searching for hidden treasure. 'They're all I ever want to eat.'

I watched her divide it into neat segments.

'How do you do that? You make it seem as easy as splitting a mandarin.'

She smiled and offered me a piece. 'I've got the fingers for it.'

I bought her a dragon fruit from the markets a few weeks later. We cut it open on her back deck.

'It looks like a rosebud,' she said, running a finger over the pink, leathery skin.

I sliced the fruit in half and she gasped at its white-and-black and speckled insides.

'Cheers.'

We clinked spoons and slurped off the pulp. Ada made a horrified face and I nodded in agreement, gulping it down as fast as possible.

'It looks a lot better than it tastes.'

I wanted to taste shockingly good. Pineapple was the fruit I ate most, hands down. I ate almost a whole pineapple every day. I ate so much pineapple that the skin round my mouth would burn and my lips would go all tingly. It made everything I drank taste fizzy. Still water was like soda water. The chopping board in our staff kitchen took on a permanently tropical smell.

'What's that, your fifth pineapple of the day?' Someone made a joke along these lines every lunchtime. If it was a co-worker I got along with, I would sometimes reply, 'Well, you know what they say about pineapple.' Apparently, none of them did. All I ever got back was a blank smile.

I tried not to draw attention to myself at work. If I stayed quiet and replied to the few emails that actually needed replies, I could get away with doing almost nothing else. This gave me a lot of time to daydream. On the few occasions someone asked me to do something, I said I hadn't been trained on that yet. I'd been working there for nearly a year, but because I was the youngest, they all assumed I didn't know how to do anything. I wasn't entirely sure what everyone else did, but it involved a lot of back and forth with the printer. Everyone spent a fair bit of the day on Facebook. Whenever I looked at my boss's computer, she was reading restaurant reviews.

I spent most of my working days that December gazing out the window at the grass and trees outside. On my break, I sat outside in the sun—reading books or arranging my slices of orange in a patch of daisies, so I could take a picture. That post got even more likes than the others.

In the weekends, I walked around in a daze. I ate nectarines, and occasionally some bread. I drank a lot of coffee. My heart was constantly beating very fast, and I felt very beautiful. I couldn't understand why no one was falling in love with me.

I didn't see many people for the first half of December. I'd expected to be spending all my time with Ada. She and I had made plans to take road trips, go night-swimming, break into an old boarding school. Instead, summer arrived and Ada stopped replying to any of my messages. I lay awake night after night, picking apart our last interactions for a reason why. I couldn't make sense of it.

When I realised I wouldn't be seeing Ada, I didn't really want to see anyone. I would have wanted to spend time with Grace, but she was close with Ada and things felt awkward between us now. Grace posted pictures of them together on Instagram, eating chips at the beach with a bunch of other friends. I liked the photos but didn't comment with a heart or a sun emoji like I would have in spring.

It was an especially hot summer. I didn't wear much clothing. My legs were constantly spotted with bruises, though I wasn't sure how I got them. I used to think bruises were ugly. I hated fruit with bruises—I was always careful to cut the bruised bits out. But since I'd started falling in love with Ada, I'd become very good at viewing my body through my imagined version of her eyes. It was like I was falling in love with myself on her behalf. Through her eyes, the bruises on my legs seemed romantic and mysterious. When I burned my hand on Grace's stove that September, the bright pink marks drew attention to how soft and vulnerable I was. Grace was horrified by the burns. I assured her they barely hurt.

In the lead-up to Christmas, stalls selling boxes of cherries popped up all over town. I wasn't crazy about cherries, though I appreciated the aesthetic. I was walking past the shops after work when I saw a stall with the prettiest cherry boxes. They were made of white cardboard, with pink and green writing, like something from the 1950s. I gave most of the cherries to my workmates, and kept the box on my bedside table, filled with the condoms I'd taken from Family Planning back in October. I'd only used three of them, and two had been with the same person.

I'd been sitting at a bar with Ada all evening. We were halfway through spring and it felt like things were finally heating up. We still hadn't kissed, but it seemed highly possible this would happen when we were out of the bar. I could feel her watching my lips when I was speaking.

We huddled over the drinks menu—our thighs occasionally brushing against each other. Ada ordered a cocktail with Cointreau and orange syrup in it.

I teased her for being so predictable. 'Oranges are not the only fruit, Ada!'

We laughed and lost our balance, nearly falling off our stools. This made us laugh harder.

While the bartender made our drinks, we did a quiz on our phones, titled 'Which Greek Goddess Are You?' I got Athena, the goddess of wisdom and war. Ada got Aphrodite.

'Aw,' said Ada. 'These are the wrong way around.'

'Are you trying to say I'm not wise?'

'No.' Ada smiled at me.

When we stepped out of the bar, it was winter cold.

'You're shivering!' Ada took off her jacket and wrapped it round me.

We paused, so close that the white clouds of our breath mingled and dissolved together.

'See you soon.' Ada waved goodbye and got on her bus.

I pulled her jacket tight across my shoulders—too exhilarated to feel any real disappointment. I'd needed to pee for about an hour but hadn't wanted to break the conversation, so now I was walking through town with an extremely full bladder. This didn't bother me. I was so happy it felt like I was glowing, and I really must have been, because when I saw Grace's friend Max across the street, he wouldn't stop staring. The two of us went to the same parties, but we'd never spoken before. He messaged me half an hour later. Since meeting Ada I had ignored all outside interest, but that night I was so full of energy I felt like I might burst if I didn't use it.

I took off Ada's jacket before going to meet him, even though it was cold. I didn't want him to touch it. My tote bag was bulky and awkward with the jacket inside. I suggested we go back to mine.

When we walked into my room, Max was distracted by all the things on my wall. I could see his eyes darting from Botticelli print to Justine Kurland photograph to *Portrait of a Lady on Fire*. Even when I took my top off, he seemed torn between looking at me or the Virgin Mary lamp on my bedside table. It wasn't until I took hold of his dick that he came fully into focus. We barely said a word to each other. When he tried to kiss me, I turned my face the other way.

We had sex again in the morning. After he left, I sat in bed eating mandarins. The sound of the segments tearing apart was more satisfying than the sex had been. I placed the wriggly peels on my sheets: their orange skin so bright against all the white. I put a photo on Instagram. @ada69 liked it within minutes.

I spent a lot of time wondering how Ada would react if I told her about Max. A part of me wanted her to find out, in the hope that she would be jealous, but when Grace asked if she should invite him to the Guy Fawkes party at her flat, I said she'd better not.

I was too excited by the possibility of Ada and I hooking

up to get any sleep the night before the party. I put on the same dress I had worn the night we met and came over early to help Grace set up, but I was so tired that I had to go lie on her bed before anyone arrived. I must have slept for a couple of hours.

I don't know whether Ada tapped me awake or my body just knew she was there. When I opened my eyes, she was looking at me with such a gentle smile.

We didn't hook up that night, although we danced as if we might. I threw back shot after shot, hoping that if I got drunk enough, I would work up the courage to make a move. She went home before I could.

Grace offered me a cap, and I swallowed it dry. When the party started winding down, I taxied into the city, determined to keep having a good time. A man in his thirties bought me a drink and we sat down in a booth. He had travelled from Russia and was only in the city for a few nights. This made me feel like I could say anything to him. When I asked what sign he was, he didn't make any of the usual comments about girls and astrology, and soon I had his full birth chart up on my phone.

'Oh, our compatibility is terrible.' I scrolled down the page. 'Except for sex and aggression.' I gave him the same smile Ada had given me.

He bought me another drink.

I tried asking him about his Myers-Briggs type, but he'd never heard of it before. After another few drinks, I folded my arms and leaned across the table. 'How do you know when you're in love?'

He raised his eyebrows. 'When you want to spend the rest of your life with that person, I guess.'

I laughed.

He looked offended. 'What would you say, then?'

'I know I'm in love when I start imagining that person watching over me all the time. Like everything I do is a performance for them.'

'Sounds creepy.'

'Creepier than buying drinks for someone ten years younger than you?'

We walked to his hostel around three. Either there wasn't a lift or the lift was broken, so we had to take the stairs. I remember me asking what floor he was on and him replying with what felt like an impossibly high number. I was so relieved when we got to his room, I didn't mind that it was the size of a wardrobe.

He gave me head for a surprisingly long time, but either he wasn't very good at it or I was too drunk to feel it properly. He had trouble staying hard, and I couldn't stop thinking how much his dick felt like a lychee, the ones you get in a can.

I went out the Saturday after Ada ghosted me, intending to take someone back to mine, but I got tired around eleven and ended up Ubering home. Instead of getting into bed, I lay down on my bedroom carpet, in the same spot Ada and I sat the last time I'd seen her. It had been the last night of November, and Grace had agreed that Ada and I would surely hook up. Everything had been leading up to this. We drank gin until the sky outside had turned from black to an eerie purple. Around midnight, I told Ada I had a crush on her. She blushed and put her hands on her cheeks.

We decided to read each other's palms. I was so distracted by the feeling of her fingers tracing my hand I could hardly take in what she was saying. It gave me a rush of ASMR— tingling swirls around my head. I can't remember what I told

Ada when I read her palm either. I do remember asking how she felt about me later in the night.

She didn't hesitate: 'Very pretty.'

This shocked me, despite the effort I always put into looking pretty around Ada. I didn't mind that she didn't say anything else.

We held on to each other's hands long after we finished the palm reading. We were both sitting cross-legged, our knees pressed together. When 'Lemon Glow' by Beach House came on, we both smiled. She moved her hands to my thighs and I did the same. Our faces were so close I could smell her breath. I expected it to smell like gin, but it was like warm milk. I could hardly breathe at all. She squeezed my knees.

'I should go home.'

Ada didn't reply to any of my texts for five days after that. When she did eventually message, it was short and vague. We fell out of touch again, but I knew I would see her at Grace's on New Year's. I planned ahead, wondering whether I should wear the same dress as the night when Ada and I met, and whether she'd recognise it. This was our chance to come full circle: everything was on hold until then.

I went through my wardrobe regularly, considering my options. I liked to believe that wearing something familiar could trigger some kind of nostalgia in her, but if I wore something shockingly different, maybe she'd pay me closer attention. I needed to look more beautiful than she remembered.

I began to collect the stickers off fruit. Apple stickers were particularly good: Eve apples, Smitten apples, Love Bite apples. I was careful about eating apples because they could make you bloat, but I liked to keep some in my room anyway. Sometimes I made an exception for the Love Bite apples. They were tangy and green—the best apples.

Green apples were Grace's favourite fruit. I used to buy them whenever I was coming over to her house, so we could cut them up and eat them in her garden. Grace was the only person who knew exactly how I felt about Ada. We used to talk on the phone while we both made dinner, and I would tell her everything that was happening and wasn't happening between Ada and me. She was a good listener, and got excited about the same things I did, but she also warned me not to get my hopes too high.

'I've seen Ada hurt people before.' A kettle whistled in the background. 'It's not that she's intentionally cruel, she's just not good at knowing what she wants.'

Even at the time, I'd known that everything Grace said was true, but still believed I could be an exception to the rule.

It felt embarrassing to talk about Ada now. The last time Grace had called was just after I'd last seen Ada. 'I'm giving up,' I'd said with a dramatic sigh, like the whole thing had been a big joke. 'She's impossible.'

'Aw,' Grace had said. 'Well, it's good you're moving on.'

A week before Christmas, Grace called to say we should catch up.

'What should I bring?' she asked.

'You don't need to bring anything.'

Grace brought black grapes and almond croissants. The last time we'd been together, Grace's hair had been dyed pastel peach. Now it was pale pink, and she'd let her roots grow out a soft brown. The brown and pink together reminded me of chocolate and strawberry milk.

Grace hugged me, but it was a loose hug—more like she was hugging the air around me than my actual body.

'How are you?' She sounded distracted.

'I'm good.'

Grace put the groceries down on the bench. 'Want a croissant?'

'I'm still pretty full from lunch. I might just eat some grapes for now.'

Grace eyed me. 'You're having one.' She opened the cupboard and took out two plates. I was surprised she remembered where we kept them, though I shouldn't have been.

'And how are you?'

Grace slid the croissants out of their little bags. The paper was soaked through with grease. 'I'm all right. Christmas shopping has bankrupted me. I hate being poor.'

I nodded, even though I had no idea what it was like to be poor. I had more in my savings than ever before, even with pineapples costing four to five dollars. Every week, more fruit came into season and the prices at the markets got cheaper. I'd been buying barely anything else.

'I can transfer you for the croissants.'

'No, don't be dumb. Consider this my Christmas present to you.'

Grace handed me a plate and sat down at the dining table. She started eating her croissant right away, and I followed obediently. It was delicious.

'So good, right?'

I nodded, wiping sticky flakes of pastry from my chin.

There was a long silence.

'Are you staying with your family over the holidays?'

'Um . . .' Grace's voice went airy, like it always did when she didn't want to talk about something. 'I'm going down for a week, yeah. Dell's back in hospital.'

'Shit, sorry. I had no idea.'

'It's fine,' she said quickly. 'I saw Ada yesterday.'

'Oh?'

'A bunch of us went blackberry picking. Ada knows this great spot. We filled, like, three jars each.'

I felt my hands clench into fists, but released them before Grace could notice. Ada had promised she would take me blackberry picking this summer. We'd even planned to make blackberry wine.

'That's nice,' I said.

'I'm going to make jam. I'll give you some.'

I nodded, pressing a slice of almond to the pad of my finger. Grace watched me. There was concern in her eyes, but I knew it was unlikely she would say anything. Grace didn't like to acknowledge things that made her, or anyone else, uncomfortable. I smiled at her and she smiled back.

'Are you sure you're okay?' she asked.

I swallowed my surprise with the last of my croissant. 'Yeah? I think so?'

'You're just so . . .' She tipped her head at me. 'Quiet.'

I shrugged. 'I've been by myself a lot.'

Grace kept looking at me. 'You know I'm—' She paused. 'Here for you.' The words sounded unnatural in her mouth. 'I know I'm useless over text, but if you ever need to talk about something . . .'

I smiled. 'I'm all good, Grace. I know how to look after myself.'

She nodded. 'I know you do.'

I tried to stay at my flat for Christmas, but Mum insisted I fly back home. The only fruit my parents ate were bananas and grapefruits. Every breakfast, I had half a grapefruit sprinkled with sugar, and a cup of black coffee. This was what my dad had eaten every morning for decades, and Mum was delighted that I had joined in the tradition. She took photos of us and sent them to our family group chat. I looked sleepy—my hair sweetly messed up and my eyes all dewy with dreaming. In one photo, I was lifting my spoon and my hand looked so beautiful I could hardly believe it was mine. My wrist floated elegantly in mid-air. My fingers were long and delicate. I posted the photo on my Instagram story and waited for Ada to see it.

Mum put me in charge of dessert for Christmas Day. I bought a watermelon so heavy I had to carry it like a baby. The skin was midnight green and satisfyingly firm. I ran my hand back and forth over its silky curve.

On Christmas morning, there was a stocking at the end of my bed. It was filled with all the same things my stocking had been filled with as a child: Pringles, bubble bath, a Terry's chocolate orange. I had bought Ada a chocolate orange back in autumn, after she told me she'd never had one. She didn't even know you had to whack it. She could hardly believe it when I peeled back the orange foil and showed her the perfect segments.

I had to use our biggest knife to cut up the watermelon. Mum hovered in the kitchen, telling me over and over to watch my fingers. It got juice all over the bench, and there were too many slices of watermelon to fit on the dessert platter. I ended up putting half of it in the fridge.

I spent most of Christmas Day dipping strawberries in melted chocolate, avoiding the rest of the family. I could hear Mum greeting everyone as they came in. Her voice strained to a higher pitch when my Aunty Cathy and her husband,

Richard, arrived. It took less than five minutes for Cathy to comment on our Christmas tree being fake. Not long after, I heard Richard interrupting someone's conversation to ask if he could take pictures of them while they were talking.

My youngest cousin, Abe, ran and jumped into my arms—nearly knocking me over. I hugged his little body awkwardly.

He sniffed. 'Your breath smells funny.'

A few older cousins wandered into the kitchen to ask me what I'd been doing this year. 'Just working,' I told them.

Louis pinched the sleeve of my jumper. 'How can you still have a jersey on? It's so hot!' Everyone else was wearing singlets and shorts.

It took a lot of effort to resist checking my phone, but I knew Mum would tell me off if I did. She'd already made a comment about me being anti-social that morning. 'You're acting so quiet. Where's my daughter gone?'

We all sat in the living room for presents. I got three soap sets. Abe got a 'Grow your own crystals' kit.

'That's cool, Abe.'

He snatched the box away. 'It's mine.'

At lunchtime, multiple aunties asked if I had a boyfriend back home. I shook my head. The aunty sitting next to me offered the potato gratin, and I explained I was trying to go vegan. She chuckled and dug her elbow into me. 'I wish I had your self-control.'

We drank wine and everyone settled into their separate conversations. I sat at the dining table amidst everyone's leftovers and torn-up paper crackers. The watermelon slices looked mostly untouched. No one but me had eaten any. Liquid pooled in the bottom of the platter, and the pink flesh had faded to a salmon colour.

I wondered whether I should message Ada a merry

Christmas. I had been wondering about this for days. I typed out a message with three strawberry emojis at the end. I hit send. My phone buzzed a little later and I jumped on it, but it was just Grace wishing me happy holidays. Ada replied on Boxing Day.

I mostly slept through the last days of December, but I set an alarm for the morning of the New Year's party. When I got out of bed, I almost felt like I was flying—my body was so light after all that time under a duvet and blanket. In the kitchen, I cut open a mango and sliced it into cubes, peeling them off the skin. When I'd bought the mango its skin had been completely green, but while I'd slept it had tinged red and orange, like a traffic light. The chunks of fruit were slippery in my mouth and slid down my throat easily. I made a plunger of coffee and took it into my room, filling and refilling my cup until my hands were shaky and jaw clenched.

I took my clothes from the wardrobe and tried on combination after combination, dumping the rejects in one pile and the potentials in another. My clothes felt looser, more comfortable than usual. At some point I started to feel dizzy and had to lie down. I closed my eyes and waited for the nausea to pass. This took about an hour. When I got up, I had a shower and put on a silky, cream-coloured dress. I had never worn this in front of Ada.

The bus to the party gave me motion sickness. I got off two stops early and sat down on a bench, digging in my bag for the nectarine I'd been saving. It was perfectly ripe, and tasted so sweet and good it felt wrong to be eating it in the dark, in the middle of suburbia.

I dropped the fleshy stone under a tree as I walked to

Grace's house. The nerves I had warded off about the party suddenly caught up with me, and I spent the whole walk trying to script what I would say to Ada, and trying to guess what she would say back.

Grace opened the door. 'Oh my god, you look like a ghost!' She was holding a wine glass with lipstick smudged round the rim. Her cheeks and neck were already flushed.

'Thanks.' I glanced across the room and saw Ada standing with some friends in the corner, but I looked away before we could make eye contact.

Grace handed me a glass. I filled it nearly to the brim with wine.

'Want some punch?' Grace dipped a ladle into a large bowl of suspiciously brown liquid. Shrivelled mint leaves floated on top. 'I think it's got kombucha in it or something. It gets you going, though!'

I finished my glass quickly, standing and sipping while old friends talked to me and I pretended to listen. I watched Ada move around the room. She never stayed in one group for long before she got distracted and jumped to a new one. She rarely joined in on the conversation, but she listened intently to whoever was speaking. Even when she took a sip from her glass, her eyes didn't leave the speaker's face. Every time she smiled the white burst of her teeth startled me awake. I had missed that smile. She was wearing the same white pants she always wore at parties, and a soft, button-down shirt. The sleeves were rolled up to her elbows, like she was about to wash the dishes.

Grace handed me a cup of punch. 'God, she's really a tease, isn't she?' Her eyes followed Ada. 'I'm sorry she put you through all that.'

I took a sip. 'It's fine.'

'I don't think it is fine.' Grace's eyes were shining like she was going to cry. 'You know you're too good for her.'

I made a face. Grace was looking right at me now. She opened her mouth to say something just as a girl yelled her name and pulled her into a hug. Grace screamed and hugged her back.

I focused on the punch. It was hard to tell what was in it, but I could drink it even faster than the wine. My stomach kept making weird noises. Someone turned the music up and I was relieved.

Ada went outside. If I turned my head a little, I could see her talking to a girl I didn't know.

'Do you have any resolutions?'

'Huh?' I blinked.

Grace's flatmate, Ellen, was smiling at me. 'Resolutions, for the New Year?'

'Oh.' I wondered for a moment. I'd been so focused on tonight, I'd barely considered the New Year. 'Spend more time outside?'

'Aw, you look like you already do! You've got that healthy glow.'

'Oh, thank you.' I could feel my cheeks burning up—the compliment and the alcohol working together to turn my face bright red. 'I'm going to the bathroom.'

As soon as I sat down on the toilet, I knew I was drunk. I peed slowly, staring at the bathmat while I waited for my bladder to empty. The air coming in the bathroom window was icy. It cooled the warmth in my cheeks, and the hair on my arms pricked up.

I stared at my reflection in the mirror while I washed my hands. The girl who stared back did look beautiful, but she was disturbingly unfamiliar. The more I looked the more unfamiliar she became, and the knowledge that she was me began to feel genuinely frightening. I poked my tongue out in the hope this would snap my consciousness back into my body, but seeing the girl in the mirror poke her tongue out scared me even more. I squeezed my eyes shut. I had been through this before; it had happened all the time when I was younger. I opened my eyes. The girl in the mirror and I mouthed to each other. 'You're silly!' We laughed. We pouted and smiled and did doe eyes. 'I'm going to talk to Ada,' we mouthed. 'I'm very pretty and I'm going to talk to Ada.' We leaned in and kissed the glass, leaving a single ghost-pink lip print.

I poured myself another drink in the kitchen, then walked outside.

'Hey, Ada.'

'Hey!' Ada turned from the people she was talking to, so we were facing each other. I could tell from the way she was smiling that she was drunk too. We stared at each other without saying anything. She really was beautiful—I hadn't made that up.

'What's been going on in your world?' she asked. Her voice was husky, and the more she drank the huskier it would become. I loved her voice when it got like this.

'Not much. Oh, I've been eating stone fruit in the shower!'

'Oh, how lovely! What do you think?'

'I understand the hype. The heat and the fruit are a good contrast.'

'Right? And you don't have to worry about getting juice everywhere.'

The two of us grinned at each other and sipped our drinks. Nothing had changed. We drank a little faster. Ada told me about going to her grandparents' house for Christmas, and when she made me laugh, I put my hand on her arm to steady myself. She gave me a look she only ever gave me at parties. I gave the same look back.

A song came on that we both loved. I dragged her into the living room. She squeezed my hands tight. Other people were dancing but I was past the point of noticing who they were. We did not break eye contact. I let my hand move to her ribcage, and her hands moved up my arms. We'd never let our bodies get this close before. Months of hunger rose up in me. Her fingers touched the back of my neck and I moved my hand just under her shirt. The soft shock of her stomach was so intimate I drew back, sliding my hand down to her hip. The music gave me a new kind of confidence. I mouthed the lyrics to her and she mouthed them back. I could smell her clean, grassy smell, and it rushed me back to spring, to first meeting her. The song ended. We hesitated before breaking apart.

'Shall we . . .'

My mind flooded. 'Okay.'

She hurried upstairs and I followed—my body buzzing with nervous anticipation. Grace's bedroom door was open. We stepped in and Ada closed it behind us. The room was full of moonlight. We were kissing before I could process what was happening. Her lips were soft, like mandarin flesh. My body pressed against the wall and Ada's body pressed into mine. My hands went numb. The only way I could tell they were still there was by holding on to Ada's waist. Every time we drew apart, she was smiling like I had never seen her smile before. This surprised me much more than the kiss.

We moved to Grace's bed. I leaned back on the pillows, and Ada crawled over me. Everything was blurred. At some point I heard cheering from downstairs and knew it must be midnight.

Ada pulled back. Her smile surprised me again. She tucked some of my hair behind my ear. 'You're so beautiful.'

Her words repeated over and over. I could feel the back of her bra under a thin layer of cotton. I kissed her neck and her breathing changed. I loved hearing her breathe like this. I undid the first few buttons of her shirt. Ada kissed along my collarbone and I heard my own breathing change to match hers. She kissed down my body, over my clothes. She stopped when she got to my hips. She put her hands on my thighs.

'I should check the time.' She sat up and got her phone out of her pocket.

I tried to orient myself.

'Oh, it's so late!' She sounded shocked. 'I should call an Uber.'

I had no idea how much time had passed. I wished she would stay longer, but speaking didn't feel possible. The blue light of Ada's phone lit her face as she tapped at the screen. I sat up. She put the phone down on the bed. We both looked at it. Her Uber would be here in seven minutes. We started kissing again. There was a new urgency to it. Her hands ran up and down my legs and I gripped her arms. I gently bit her lip, then harder. She bit mine back.

Her phone buzzed. I let her go. I watched, blinking, as she hopped off the bed, buttoned her top up again and straightened her hair. She was still smiling.

'See you.' She closed the door behind her.

I stood up from the bed. I felt light-headed. I lay back down and tried to breathe slowly. My heart was beating with a violence I wasn't used to—hard and loud. When I put my hands on my tummy I could feel it doing little jumps with every beat. My stomach was soft and sunken. I ran my fingers over my hip bones and replayed everything that had just happened. Some memories made my whole body jolt. I'd imagined it a million times, but the details astounded me. I had never imagined an afterwards. There was a drug-like happiness, similar to the feeling I had when I woke up from a dream about Ada, but there was also a sickness, a slipping away, a sealing off. I could feel myself falling from one dream state into another. In my mind, someone was opening the door.

On my third night in Queenstown, we went to watch Maddison's childhood crush play at Blue Door. We let strangers buy us quadruple-shot gin and tonics until we were so drunk we had to hold on to each other for balance. We danced with our hands on each other's arms and waists. If I let Maddison go, I was sure she would fall. When 'Valerie' played, we sang every word.

The band took us back to their place. Maddison's childhood crush got out his guitar and said he was going to play for us girls. He sang 'If You Want to Sing Out, Sing Out' by Cat Stevens in a high-pitched American accent.

I looked at Maddison and watched all the love she'd had for him dissolve. I looked away, knowing if she and I made eye contact we would start giggling.

In the morning, we woke up before any of the boys. We got an Uber home without saying goodbye, and laughed about them the whole ride.

ASCENDANT—OUTER APPEARANCE—
GEMINI(?)/TAURUS

Maddison's birth certificate says she was born on 24 August, but her mum insists she was born the next day. This means her rising and moon signs will always be dubious. These are our two differing placements.

If Maddison was born when her mum says, her ascendant is in Gemini. Gemini risings come across as curious and fun, but also inconsistent. Maddison often finds that people don't recognise her, even when they've met her multiple times before. We blame her hair. It is constantly changing. Over the years, I have seen Maddison's hair pink most often, but I have also seen it blonde, orange, dark brown, pastel purple and bright purple. I have seen it blue and purple mixed. Whenever I listen to 'Pink Purple Blues', I think of her hair. There is a purple stain on the wall behind her bed from where she leaned her head too soon after dyeing it.

I have never seen her hair in its natural state, but sometimes it creeps in at the roots: a milky brown, the same colour as her eyelashes.

MOON—MOOD & EMOTIONS—
TAURUS(?)/SAGITTARIUS

Maddison is either a Gemini moon or a Taurus moon. She identifies as the latter—meaning we both have major Taurus placements. Tauruses are grounded in the physical world: they take pleasure in the five senses. Maddison and I always surround ourselves with good smells. We buy luxury candles, Parisian perfume, lavender pillows. When I stayed with her in Queenstown, we slept in a caravan she had filled with flowers. Most of them were lilies. The smell was so intense that it woke me up in the night, but I was happy to lie awake breathing it in.

Back in Wellington, Maddison's bedroom smells of sweet vape clouds: strawberry milk, menthol, vanilla. During summer, she bought a yuzu-passionfruit flavour that smells exactly like Polly Pockets. Whenever I'm with her, I ask for a sip and she passes the vape to me. Sometimes she repeats the word 'sip' and laughs.

We both love taking naps. Much of our time together is spent lying in Maddison's bed—drifting in and out of sleep, listening to our shared Spotify playlists. We like 'Luxurious' by Gwen Stefani, with its lyrics about Egyptian cotton.

Maddison and I both adore expensive things. We spend

hundreds of dollars on skincare: rose-scented toners and tubes of French moisturiser. We order five-course meals, and go out for fancy Japanese lunches, where they give you a hot flannel to clean your hands before eating. I always let Maddison pick the wine, because she works at a natural wine bar and knows what I like. I will spend far more money splitting a bottle with Maddison than I would with anyone else. I love seeing her get excited.

I come to Maddison's house on Saturday mornings, before she has woken up, and climb onto her bed with a box of macarons or almond croissants. When there's Ferrero Rochers at work, I steal her a few. She makes me Russian honey cake, topped with handfuls of chopped pistachios. I make her gnocchi from scratch—fried in sage butter and garlic.

We haven't always been like this. When we met, we drank our coffee black and tried to eat vegan. We never lined our stomachs before drinking, and ended up vomiting in pot plants and Ubers. Now, we keep an eye on each other. I remind Maddison that even though she works nights and sleeps until the afternoon, she still needs to eat three meals. When we're making toast after a party and I say I only want one piece, Maddison gives me two. I tell her that, according to medical astrology, the stomach and digestive system are ruled by Virgo.

VENUS—LOVE & PLEASURE—LIBRA/LIBRA

In the spring of 2019, I slept over in Maddison's bed every weekend. We stayed up talking about my new crush, and whether I should break up with my boyfriend. When I finally did, Maddison said I could stay with her until I found a new flat. She and I were both working full-time:

me in a library and her in a wine bar. Each night, I tucked myself into her bed, slept for a few hours, then woke up again when she got home. Sometimes she was drunk off the glasses of wine that customers had shouted her. We lay there chatting about my day and her night—our legs tossed over each other. After my boyfriend and I broke up, she and I were always touching: my fingers in her hair, her hands running up and down my arms. Most nights we talked until my alarm went off. I spent the daytime high on lack of sleep, and napped on the grass outside the library on my lunch break. Sometimes Maddison came by to deliver me a macaron or an iced maple.

On Halloween, Maddison and her flatmates threw a party. We were both hoping to make out with our crushes, but while we were getting ready we agreed, 'If neither of us pull, we'll make out instead.' I couldn't tell if she was joking. I wasn't sure if I was either. I dressed up as the not-so-Virgin Mary and Maddison was a milkmaid. Neither of us pulled. We lay in bed whispering, like we did most nights, but our bodies were even closer than usual.

MARS—SEX & AGGRESSION—SCORPIO/SCORPIO

Maddison and I had only had sex with men before we slept with each other. We agreed afterwards that it was some of the best sex either of us had ever had. The second time we slept together, fireworks went off. We were in my bed and FKA Twigs was playing.

When we heard the fireworks, Maddison pulled away to ask, 'Is that part of the music, or is that real?' She was grinning.

I told her it was real and we kept kissing.

Afterwards, I lay with my face on her lower stomach while she scratched my head.

'Sex is actually great, isn't it?'

I nodded, my head bumping her hip. 'Yeah, it's the best.'

Maddison hummed. Her skin smelled of bar soap.

'But I've been lucky,' I added.

Maddison and I both kept sleeping with other people after we started sleeping together. We talked about this over dinner in an expensive restaurant. We hadn't seen each other for nearly two weeks, and soon realised that over that time we had both hooked up with 32-year-old Taurus men. We held hands over the table, cracking up at the coincidence.

We finished our first wine and started on the second.

Maddison put down her glass. 'Joy, I think I've got a problem having actual feelings towards people I'm dating.'

I laughed. 'No shit.'

'What! You knew that already?'

'I feel like we talk about this all the time.'

'Damn. Well, I've been thinking about how I've only been in one relationship, and how toxic it got . . . and I've realised it probably traumatised me!'

'Yeah, isn't that why you've avoided any sort of relationship for two years?'

Maddison nodded in disbelief. 'I can't believe you already know all this.'

'It makes sense. And your childhood probably plays a part too. Parents teach you how to love and all that.'

Maddison swallowed a mouthful of wine. 'Yeah, true.'

I grinned. 'Or maybe you're just a Gemini moon.'

—

Scorpio placements are known to be secretive and obsessive. I am not particularly secretive, but I am definitely obsessive. I tell Maddison I am obsessed with her, in person and in the letters I write. I talk about Maddison all the time—to all the people in my life. I tell them she is one of my favourite people in the world.

Maddison is not particularly obsessive, but she is secretive. There is a part of her life she barely ever talks about. When she first told me, I held her body very tight to mine. We made pinkie promises.

We've talked about it a few times since then, always when we are lying in the dark. Sometimes we wonder about the ways it might have shaped who Maddison is now, but mostly this feels boring and inaccurate.

'That's one of the reasons I don't tell people about it,' Maddison says.

We agree it's more fun to blame things on your birth chart than on the bad things that have happened to you.

MERCURY—INTELLECT & COMMUNICATION
—VIRGO/VIRGO

Maddison's favourite emoji is the love letter emoji. She has only ever written me one letter, and in it she tells me to please continue reading her poems and stories, and that I should also write some about her. I tell her it's hard to write about something so good. She asks if she should cause some conflict and I roll my eyes.

I have written her many letters and many cards. In them, I tell her how unbelievably lucky I feel to have what we have together. I tell her she is so smart and so strong and I am so proud of her. I tell her, *Fetch the bolt cutters, baby!*

Three of these cards are blu-tacked to Maddison's wall, along with a matchbox I made for her, with a little moon on it. Every full moon in Virgo, I send a text wishing her a wonderful night.

URBAN FORAGING

First it's just seaweed. Wallace is doing their honours project on foraging at Wellington beaches, and I have come along with them to Moa Point. I sit on a rock in a sheer nightgown while Wallace passes me starfish and a sea slug the size of a human head. They take photos of the creatures in my hands. Sometimes I feel them getting the rest of me in the picture too. The whole day already feels like a memory, and I am glad they are capturing it. I hold their camera for them as they climb down into the water.

'Did you know there are around eight hundred species of seaweed in New Zealand?' they say. 'And basically all of them are edible.'

I find the taste of seaweed so off-putting that I sometimes peel it off sushi, but I haven't mentioned this to Wallace.

They lift up what looks like a string of green olives. 'Neptune's necklace.'

They pass it to me. The sea-beads are more like grapes than olives, rubbery and hard to pop.

Wallace fills a net bag with wakame, kelp, sea lettuce.

'Could we make skincare with any of these?' they ask.

'Um,' I say. 'You can use dried seaweed as an exfoliant. And

I know how to do a carrageenan infusion, for a face mask.'

'Could we use kelp instead?'

'Maybe.'

Back at Wallace's, they fill a large pot with kelp and boiling water. I don't think it's going to work, but I act like it might. They plug their camera into their laptop to transfer the photos from the beach. I want Wallace to send them to me, but don't want them to think I only get out into nature for photos' sake. Also I might look bad in them. Wallace pegs the rest of the seaweed on the washing line to dry. I sit on the deck, trying to watch them without getting sun in my eyes.

Next time we're on the deck, Wallace is rinsing kina. They've been diving at the beach while Celeste and I were sleeping in. Celeste has never eaten kina, but she's promised Wallace that she'll try it.

'Is that blood?' I ask, staring at the red stuff all over Wallace's hands.

Wallace grins up at me. 'Do you want to try one?' They say it like a dare.

Celeste kicks them. 'She's a proper vegetarian, remember?'

'Oh, yeah.'

A part of me wants Wallace to keep pushing it. I would try the kina if they wanted me to. This is one of many things I would do for Wallace that I would never do for anyone else.

'It looks like a brain.' Celeste leans over and pokes at the orange flesh. It moves.

'Are you sure you want to eat that hungover?' I ask.

'I'll be all right.'

Wallace cuts up a lemon stolen from the neighbour's garden and squeezes it over the kina. I make them both wait for me to swipe into my camera and hit record before they eat. It's thrilling to video Wallace. They throw back the kina like a tequila shot. Celeste eats more carefully. Her reaction is underwhelming. The clip ends with me saying, 'Aw.'

Celeste goes inside to have a shower.

Wallace picks up the shell holding the last of the meat. 'Are you sure you don't want to try?'

I take the shell and swirl the flesh around. 'What does it taste like?'

'Have you tried scallops?'

'I've never had any kind of shellfish. It's been five years since I ate fish-fish.'

'Wow. I guess it tastes like fish-fish.'

I sniff it, but I can mostly smell the lemon. I look at Wallace. 'Give me a good reason to eat it.'

They think for a minute. 'I'll make you elderflower cordial? There's heaps growing up in Melrose.'

The kina flesh pulses.

'I'm scared.'

They smile at me. 'No pressure, you really don't have to—'

I swallow it without chewing. It tastes all wrong: like a fish milkshake. I make a face and Wallace laughs with delight.

Wallace and I add gin to the elderflower cordial and drink it in Central Park. They look so pretty in the long, waving grass that I almost ask to take a picture, but I back out. It's easier to look at each other if we don't acknowledge that we're doing it.

Wallace points up at a pine tree and tells me about the time they nearly killed themself climbing one, in a mission to forage their own pine nuts.

'You're supposed to let the pine cones dry out, but we couldn't be bothered waiting three weeks, so we put them in the oven. Then you're supposed to tap out the nuts and put them in a bowl of water. The ones that are good to eat will sink to the bottom. Then you shell them.'

'That's a lot of work,' I say.

'Yeah. Anyway, they all floated to the top.'

We find wild blackberries, though they shouldn't be in season yet.

'Must be global warming,' I say.

We both put one in our mouth. They're bitter and underripe.

'It's like eating soap!' I say, spitting mine out.

When I spot a patch of periwinkles, I ask Wallace if they've ever seen a fairy toothbrush. They shake their head. I pick one of the purple flowers and peel back the petals—taking care not to crush the tiny white stem hidden in its centre. Once it's free, I pinch it between two fingers and hold it in the air. The stem is about the same length as my pinkie fingernail. The flower at the top is smaller than a sesame seed: white and yellow.

'Oh, it actually does look like a toothbrush!' Wallace holds their hand out and I pass it to them. They twirl the stem between the tips of their fingers.

The next morning, a woman is stabbed in Central Park while walking her dog. I tell my friends, 'We were there the day before,' in the same way Wallace talked about nearly falling from the pine tree, but when I tell Wallace, they seem genuinely frightened.

'She's okay,' I reassure them. 'She got stitches.'

Wallace won't come to Central Park after that. I know I should at least be scared out of walking through the park alone, but I keep doing it. It doesn't feel any more dangerous than it did before. I walk through the park drunk, in the dark, with my headphones in. When I walk past the pine tree, I think, 'I could never climb that.'

Celeste drives the three of us up to Wallace's uncle's farm. It's just over an hour out of the city. We see fields of sheep on the way.

'Look! Baby lambs!' My voice comes out high-pitched, like a child's.

Wallace shakes their head, exasperated. 'They're just lambs!'

Wallace's Uncle Peter greets us at the gate with his border collie, Maisy. 'Good to see you, my girl,' he says, whacking Wallace on the back.

Celeste and I glance at each other.

Peter raises his eyebrows when I get out of the car wearing a knee-length white dress and maroon-coloured boots, but I enjoy looking out of place. We go into the farmhouse and Wallace's Aunty Jane immediately offers to lend me a pair of gumboots. I decline and Wallace smiles at the ground.

'It's so nice to meet some of Wallace's friends.' Jane puts one hand on Celeste's shoulder and the other on mine. 'Who needs a boyfriend when you've got friends, hey girls?'

Wallace avoids eye contact with either of us.

'True,' I say.

Jane and Celeste talk in the kitchen while I go to the pond with Wallace and Peter. Celeste's seen her brothers shoot ducks before and knows she doesn't like it. I suspect I won't like it either, but I'm fascinated to watch Wallace. When they come out holding a shotgun, I find them even hotter than usual.

'Can I hold it?' I ask.

I take the gun from Wallace very carefully, afraid I will somehow touch it wrong and end up shooting something. It's lighter than I expect. It seems too slim and smooth to be capable of killing.

After five minutes of walking, my boots are more mud-brown than maroon. Only the ankles remain their original colour. Wallace points this out and I shrug. 'Most of it will wash off.'

They look concerned.

'I like the mud-stain aesthetic,' I reassure them.

The duck pond is not what I expect. I realise I was picturing something like the one at the Botanic Gardens, but this pond is massive. I can't see an end to it.

Wallace lifts their shotgun. They turn slightly, and for a moment I think they're going to point it at me. A rapid fire of images floods my vision: bullets shooting into eyeballs, fingers flying off, my body dead in the leaves. I clench my jaw and try not to flinch.

Peter sends Maisy off to scare the ducks. She disappears into the brushes and flax, but we can hear her barking. The ducks rise up off the water and into the sky. It's muggy and overcast. Wallace and Peter sit their shotguns against their shoulders and stand very still, carefully directing each barrel to follow the ducks' flight.

I watch Wallace pull the trigger. The butt kicks back so hard into their shoulder I'm surprised they don't fall to the ground. My body jumps for them. Flocks of birds fly up from the trees at the sound of the gunshot. It reverberates in my ears. The hills are ringing and the air smells of gunpowder. It takes me back to Guy Fawkes parties—setting off fireworks and sprinting away, chasing my cousins around with sparklers.

'Did you hit anything?' I ask.

'It's hard to know, from this distance,' Wallace says. 'Maisy will find it if we did.'

Wallace and Peter shoot a few more rounds. I watch a duck fall from the sky, but we're too far to hear it hit the ground.

'Do you want a go?' Wallace gestures at the shotgun. 'I can teach you.'

I stutter out a 'No thanks.'

'Don't worry, you don't have to aim at the ducks.' Wallace's tone is caring, but I can hear the challenge.

I shake my head. 'I'm okay.'

Celeste wants to try mushroom tea on her birthday, so Wallace and I go up to Mount Victoria to pick some. It's a cold morning. The air is damp and dewy. My cotton sundress provides very little warmth, and when Wallace offers me their Swanndri, I accept. I pull it carefully over my head, trying not to mess up my hair.

Wallace is smiling at me. 'You look cute.'

I wish I could check in a mirror to confirm this, but I do like wearing the Swanndri. Somehow, I feel even more feminine in Wallace's clothes than I do in my own.

'Did I tell you about Marina and the watermelon peperomias?' I say, as we walk between the pine trees.

Wallace says no.

'She took me with her to the Begonia House to body-shield her while she stole cuttings. She sells them on Facebook marketplace. Twenty-five dollars a leaf.'

Wallace laughs, impressed. 'You should ask for a cut.'

There are lots of mushrooms above the bus tunnel. Before we touch any, Wallace checks them against a series of pictures to make sure we're getting the right ones.

'These ones are deadly,' Wallace says, pointing at the cluster of mushrooms on their phone screen. They look identical to the ones we're crouched over: shiny brown caps, long creamy stems. Wallace swipes to the next image. These mushrooms look the same too. 'And these ones are golden tops.

That's what we want.'

Wallace inspects the mushrooms, comparing them closely to the pictures. I'm disturbed by how similar they all look. When Wallace is satisfied, they tear the mushrooms out of the earth and place them in one of the paper bags we've brought along.

'We'll do a spore print tonight, anyway.' They tuck the bag into their jacket pocket. 'If the print turns purple-brown, we're good.'

We wander further up the hill, filling two more bags on the way.

'My friend Rosa found a dead body around here, back in year ten,' I say. I'm not sure where the words come from. I haven't thought about this in years.

Wallace looks startled. 'Really?'

'Yeah, right up by our school. Rosa was on a run with her dad. This guy came rushing up to them saying a woman was hurt, then he ran off. They found her body a few metres off the path. Rosa only saw a glimpse before her dad told her to stay back.'

'What happened to her? The woman, I mean.'

'They never figured it out. She had a history of inhalant abuse, but the autopsy only showed trace amounts.'

My eyes are focused on the ground, but I can feel Wallace staring at me. 'Were you and your friends scared?'

I pause before speaking. 'It just didn't seem real. Not even to Rosa, I think.' I kick a rock off the track. 'It's hard to imagine something like that actually happening to you.'

Neither of us say anything for a while. The leaves whisper under our feet as we walk. We turn a corner and come to a small clearing. Wallace gasps before I have time to spot the fairy ring. A split second later, my gasp echoes theirs.

When they turn to look at me, their whole face is radiating excitement. I've never seen them so happy.

Wallace leans close to look at the mushrooms. They're unevenly spaced, but they're definitely in a circle. They have much flatter, paler tops than the golden caps. Wallace swipes into their camera and takes a few photos of the individual mushrooms, then jumps up again.

'Go stand in the middle!' they say, running back so they can get the whole circle in the shot.

'It's bad luck to step inside a fairy ring,' I call out. 'I might disappear into another world.'

'Come on!' Wallace calls back. They've climbed onto a dead log and have their camera ready. 'If you disappear, I'll come in after you.'

I step right to the edge of the fairy ring. I know I must be making it up, but it feels like there's a forcefield pushing me back, urging me to stay out. Even the birdsong from the forest sounds like a warning. I look at Wallace and they're grinning at me. I step inside.

MATERIAL GIRL

You were proud of the fact that you didn't have much stuff. You told me you weren't a minimalist, but you'd read a book on minimalism, and wrote a list of the points you found interesting or helpful. Your bedroom was very small and almost empty. Aside from the few photos blu-tacked to your wall, everything had a function.

The first time you came to my house, I wondered if you would judge me for all my little things: the anatomically correct heart candle, the vintage drinking glass with the signs of the zodiac printed on it, the baby pink telephone I bought purely for decoration. I knew you would approve of the crystals and geodes, and the dried flowers hanging in the window, because these were things from nature. I shuffled my stacks of books so Gabriela Mistral and Adrienne Rich were on the top. I stuffed my make-up bag into a drawer.

You walked around my room like it was a museum— asking permission before you touched anything. If you lingered on something, I would tell you its history. *That was my mum's, from before I was born. My friend painted that for me in high school.* You smelled all my perfumes and bottles of skincare from Parisian apothecaries. You asked how many

Virgin Marys I thought I had. *Around twenty-seven.* You told me about all the Marys your mum had back home, and all the Marys at your grandparents' house, in Chile. *But not as many as this.*

You slipped your hands into my red leather gloves with the heart cut out on the back and wiggled your fingers. You went through my record collection and pulled out the albums you liked: Lana Del Rey, FKA Twigs, Françoise Hardy. When you found the Florence + the Machine record with 'St Jude' on it, you asked me to put it on. I went to the bathroom before the song finished, and when I came back I found you reading *An Atlas of Natural Beauty.*

We drank gin I had infused with cinnamon quills, vanilla and tonka beans. You told me about the perfume at Aesop that you wanted but wouldn't buy. I asked why not. *I'm bad at letting myself have the things I want,* you said.

The sky turned to night. I put on my red, heart-shaped wall light and lit a cedar-scented candle. The tiny plastic ponies lined up on my windowsill glowed in the dark.

You inspected the cards and drawings pinned to my wall. *Do you keep all the letters people write you?*

I nodded. *What about you?*

I just take a photo. Then I throw them out.

That's fucked up. I tried to sound like I was joking, but some genuine horror crept into my voice. The note you had written me was glued in my journal.

We drank more gin. You pointed at my pink heels with the red soles, also shaped like hearts. *Heart trotters,* you said. You picked up my platforms with the LED screen you code messages into, and pushed the 'on' button. 'MATERIAL GIRL' scrolled across the screen, from the last party I'd worn them to. You asked to try on my white thigh-high boots with the stars and the moons embroidered on them. You strutted around the room and I lay down laughing.

You asked what I would save first if the house was on fire. I opened up the teal suitcase where I kept all my old diaries, and let you look at them. *Don't open any though*, I said quickly.

There's so many. Your voice was full of awe. These were the best proof I had that I wasn't only a material girl. I wanted you to wonder what was inside.

You grinned, holding up a spiral-bound diary with Tracey Beaker on the cover. *That's from when I was ten,* I said. I watched you run your hands over green leather journals and cloth-bound notebooks. I was startled by how intimate this felt. *I've never let anyone do this before,* I told you.

You left around 3am. When you were gone, I got down on my knees and prayed to all my Virgin Mary figurines. *Please let me have what I want.*

Over the next few weeks, we started exchanging books. Before lending anything, I would reread it myself—underlining the best bits. I wrote dates and initials next to sections that reminded me of a certain time or a certain person, but never your initials. Sometimes I would draw a heart or an exclamation mark next to lines that reminded me of you, hoping you would figure it out.

We gave each other a few small things. I stuck four scented matchsticks in the skeleton doll that hung on your bedroom door. I made you a matchbox with a picture of an orange on it. You hand painted me the two tarot cards that align with my birthday: 'Strength' and 'The Star'. I stuck them to my bedroom door.

I spent a lot of time wondering about Christmas. Gift-giving was your lowest ranking love language, but maybe if

I got you something good it would make you love me a little bit. Recently, you'd shown me a gift from your ex that you kept hidden in your wardrobe. I didn't want to be hidden in the wardrobe. I wanted to give you something you would look at every day, something you could keep forever. I wanted you to have the perfume from Aesop, but I knew I couldn't buy you something so expensive. I decided to get you a selection of smaller gifts. Most of them were things you could use, but my favourites were the two tiny bottles of scented oil from a New Age store, labelled 'Gemini' and 'St Jude'.

I made you an especially pretty card and sprayed it with my perfume—hoping this would lessen the chances of you taking a photo of it and throwing it away. In the card, I said *I hope I see you lots in the year to come.* I debated over whether or not to sign it with 'love'. In the end I just wrote my name.

We agreed to exchange gifts at my house the night before you went back to your parents'. You came over around midnight, even though your flight was at 8am. You gave me an unwrapped bottle of gin, no card. I gave you your presents all wrapped in a single parcel, and your card tucked into an envelope.

Should I open it now?

I shook my head. *I'll feel too uncomfortable. Save it for Christmas Day.*

We talked on my floor—holding hands and staring at each other—for a long time. I confessed that I'd also made you a playlist, but I'd been hesitant to share it with you.

Maybe I'll send it tomorrow.

You should. I have a playlist for you too.

At 3am, I asked if I could kiss you. You left around four.

I sent you the playlist when I woke up the next day. You followed it but didn't send one back. I listened to the playlist over and over, trying to figure out whether it was too much, whether I'd scared you off. You didn't text on Christmas. You didn't text until New Year. You had just found my gift in the midst of your unpacking, and thanked me for all the lovely things.

We didn't see each other in January. You ignored most of my texts, and when I tried to make plans, you always cancelled at the last minute. I kept myself busy and mostly distracted, but when I bought a Virgin Mary candle holder that cried wax tears out of her eyes, you were the first person I wanted to show. When I read *A Manual for Cleaning Women*, I drew stars next to the stories set in Chile and imagined lending it to you. When I spent seventy dollars on a wicker bag shaped like a house—with a tiny front door that opened up—I wondered if you would approve.

I got a drink with your flatmate, and she said you'd applied for a job in another city but didn't get it. *They still talk about you a lot. I always hear them listening to that playlist you made.*

I came round to your house at the end of summer, and aside from a brief hello, you and I ignored each other. I walked past your open bedroom door as I was leaving. The 'Gemini' and 'St Jude' bottles were positioned carefully on your bedside table.

I moved into a flat with an attic bedroom, just like I'd told you I wanted. We hadn't spoken in months. I felt sure you would like the flowers in our garden, the sloping ceilings, the carpeted staircase—so steep and narrow it was almost like a ladder. My door frame was so low the moving guys had to dip their heads whenever they came in or out, but you'd have stepped under it no problem. You were barely any taller than me.

It took me almost a week to unpack all my things from their boxes and bubble wrap. This room was much smaller than my last one: I knew it wasn't all going to fit. I went through everything one by one—putting some in storage, giving some away, throwing a few out. I was surprised by how easy it was to narrow them down.

June arrived, and your birthday with it. I thought about the gifts I would have bought you: face masks made of clay and dried strawberry powder, Spanish tarot cards, the photobook of all Frida Kahlo's possessions. I couldn't decide whether or not I should text you. I did it anyway. You texted me a thank you, then texted again the next day. You came round to my flat with a twig of mānuka in your hand. You tucked it in the vase of jasmine I'd positioned on our coffee table. I gave you a flat tour. In my room, you asked questions about the things you hadn't seen before. *My sister made me that for Christmas,* I said, as you touched your finger to the record pinned on my wall: painted with my nickname and pictures of fruit. You slid *Titanic Rising* out of my new lilac record crate and stared at the underwater bedroom on the cover.

We sat together on my bed. *I bought the Aesop perfume,* you said, holding out your wrist. I cupped my hand round it and breathed in yuzu, basil, and vetiver. *I'm happy for you,* I said.

After you left, I took the mānuka twig out of the vase and held it in my palm. It was mostly leaves: there were only two tiny red flowers. I liked to imagine that was why you'd picked it, but doubted you'd thought about this at all.

MORAL DELINQUENCY
IN CHILDREN
AND ADOLESCENTS

The girls sneak out of school for the thrill of it. Lunchtime's only an hour and the milk bar's too far away, so they head up Mount Victoria and into the forest. They hang their school ties on a tree branch. They line up their shoes underneath, with their stockings stuffed inside. On hot days they peel off their pinafores, too—down to their school blouses and the white cloth knickers they wear for gym.

Caroline and Rosemary take their notebooks and pencils up to the grass clearing where the rope swing used to be. Nobody tries to join them. They pick honeysuckle on the way—taking only the yellowest flowers, because these taste the sweetest. They pinch the stem between their nails and squeeze the tiny droplets of nectar onto each other's tongues. In the clearing, Rosemary writes and Caroline draws pictures of her writing. They hum the same songs and can't figure out who started humming first.

Margaret holds court on an old tree stump. She tells the girls about the Naenae boys and the Petone gang and the party she went to in Lower Hutt. She tells them about the water fountains and the tanks full of tropical fish at Elbe's milk bar. She tells them about the French letters you can buy under the counter at the High Street chemist, and the knife fight she saw on the weekend. When she's out of stories, they all play hide and seek. They climb trees and scramble into bushes and lie down flat behind a fallen log. They breathe shallow and silent. The youngest girl keeps an eye on her wristwatch to make sure they're not late for class.

On their way back, the girls spot Bruce and Diane coming down from the forest too. The two of them have been going steady for more than three months now. Bruce is eighteen years old and rides a motorcycle. Diane is sixteen and has blonde curls that fall to the bottom of her back. The two of them are so beautiful they look like something out of a movie or a fairy-tale. Bruce picks the leaves out of Diane's hair and kisses her goodbye at the school gates. The bell rings.

Diane sings the hymn in assembly, but she doesn't think about the words. She thinks about how her body feels pressed against Bruce when she's on the back of his motorcycle, the Brylcreem smell of his hair. While Miss Wilson reads from the Bible, Diane thinks about Bruce's hand on her thigh in the back row of the picture theatre, the *Creature from the Black Lagoon* rising up from the screen's watery darkness. She thinks about his fingers reaching the clasp on her garter belt.

Miss Wilson switches into her scolding voice. She's talking about the uniform: girls have been spotted in public without their gloves and hats on. If this continues, there will be no mufti day. Her tone turns even harsher as she reminds the girls that talking to boys on street corners is strictly forbidden— especially boys on motorcycles. The girl sitting next to Diane shoots her a grin.

Diane feels her face going pink. During the school song, she imagines sitting in Miss Wilson's office explaining that

Bruce isn't a bodgie, he's just a boy, the only boy. She knows no matter what she says, Miss Wilson won't believe her. The girls stare at their lap for the Lord's Prayer.

Diane thinks back to the holidays, to all the time they spent in the sand. She thinks about Bruce squeezing lemon juice into her hair, so that it would go light in the sun. She thinks about him kissing the juice off her forehead and temples. She can almost smell the citrus.

In biology Margaret finds the anatomy book with the green cover and turns to page 97: the reproductive system. None of the girls can much understand the diagram of the female organs, but the male ones are what they're interested in anyway. A group gathers round as Margaret takes a measuring tape and wraps it round a glue stick, for comparison. One of the girls shouts, 'Ouch!', and Miss Jones looks up from her marking. She whips the book out of Margaret's hands. As she takes in the diagram, the Y-shaped vein in the middle of her forehead bulges like it's going to burst.

'Are you *sick*?' she says to Margaret. 'Do you need to go to the *sick bay*?'

The girls stare hard at the Formica tabletop and just manage not to laugh.

'Out.'

Miss Jones points at the door and Margaret doesn't even sigh. The only teachers who don't kick her out of class are Mademoiselle Bélanger and Miss Mayer. Miss Mayer teaches English, and she's everyone's favourite. She weeds the rock garden with them on the last day of term, and never scolds Margaret for wearing white nail polish.

While the other girls are getting changed for gym, Margaret tells Miss Dixon she's got stomach cramps.

Miss Dixon raises her eyebrows. 'You're the first young lady I've ever known to get her period more than once a month, Margaret.' She lets her sit out anyway.

Margaret walks up above the school field while Miss Dixon inspects the gym uniforms of the girls below. Three get house points taken off for dirty sandshoes. 'Please, Dicky,' they beg, but there's no use arguing. Once the class has started their exercises, Miss Dixon disappears to the staffroom. She'll be back in ten minutes, smelling of cigarettes.

Margaret watches the girls get into their first positions for drill display. They all look the same from this distance: black shorts and white blouses, hair tied back. Miss Dixon blows her whistle and they march into a large circle, then shift into a star. Margaret knows at the school gala there will be two circles and two stars, but the fifth-formers are in Math right now. There's a collective hesitation before the girls start marching into their final position, and a few of them stumble on the way. When the fifth-formers are here, their bodies will spell out the school's acronym, but for now they only spell the first half: WE.

Caroline and Rosemary don't have any classes together, but they meet by the school fountain as soon as the school day is over. On Tuesdays they walk down to Wellington College for ballroom dancing with Miss Dixon, but every other day they walk to the tram.

If Caroline's father is away, they go to her house and listen to records in the living room. Their favourite is the *Gentlemen Prefer Blondes* soundtrack. When 'Two Little Girls from Little Rock' comes on, they jump up and dance like Marilyn Monroe and Jane Russell. They watched the movie three times in the theatres last year: once at the Regent, once at the

Embassy and once at the Majestic. They know all the words.

Sometimes Caroline stops in the middle of their dancing and holds her finger up to shush Rosemary. She lifts the needle off the record and they stand frozen in silence, listening for the sound of a car pulling up, the slam of a door, footsteps, keys. Up the street, they hear the tinkle of 'Greensleeves'. They scramble for their purses and rush out to the Peter Pan truck.

If Caroline's father is home, they go to Rosemary's. Her mother doesn't let them buy ice creams, and her brothers are always using the record player, but they can hide in Rosemary's bedroom.

On Fridays and sometimes Saturdays, Caroline stays the night. There's a spare mattress under Rosemary's bed, but they never use it. Caroline asks Rosemary to read one of her stories, and Rosemary says okay, but only if she can lie with her back to Caroline—she gets too embarrassed when she can see her face. Caroline draws pictures on Rosemary's back with her finger. When she turns round, Caroline is always smiling. They talk until they're half-asleep—their faces pressed together.

The nights that they're apart, they call each other on the phone. It's in the kitchen where everyone can hear, and they're only allowed a few minutes, but they always try for longer. While they're talking they loop the long, coiled cord round and round a palm, then try to twist the coil round their index finger. When the cord pulls at the wall, they feel like they're pulling for each other.

Girls call all across the city: turning the telephone wires into a web of whispers.

—

That winter, frost clings to the telephone wires and crunches under the girls' shoes on their way to school. They're grateful for the hats and gloves they usually complain about. It's too cold to go into the forest.

The first thing Rosemary sees that morning is four girls huddled over a newspaper. She's never seen anyone bring a newspaper to school before. By the time she reaches the art block, she's seen another two, and a bunch of girls with clippings fluttering in their hands. Caroline isn't waiting for her by the water fountain.

She hears whispers of it during maths. *Fifteen and sixteen years old. A brick and a stocking.* By second period she knows it happened in Christchurch, that their names are Juliet and Pauline, that the woman they killed was Pauline's mother. By third period she knows they hit her more than twenty times. A girl shows her the article at lunch. She points at the words 'intense devotion' and 'unhealthy relationship'.

'You know what that means,' she whispers in Rosemary's ear. The article says the girls spent almost all of their time together—talking or writing stories—and often slept over in each other's beds. Their parents encouraged them to spend time with other girls, but they only wanted to be with each other.

When Rosemary calls Caroline on the phone that night, her father picks up instead. She apologises and hangs up.

All week, Rosemary catches glimpses of girls she thinks are Caroline. An art pad tucked under a sweatered arm, a golden ponytail, black stockings with ladders creeping down the calves. Caroline hasn't called, and Rosemary's scared to keep calling. She waits by the water fountain every morning and afternoon, tracing the pattern of its blue tiles with a stick. Nobody comes to meet her. She looks for Caroline in assembly, but there are so many girls with straight, sandy hair, and Rosemary's always stuck at the back. At lunch she checks the art block and the library, then walks the corridors like a maze. She doesn't know her way out.

The girls can't stop talking about the murder. 'They're the same age as us.' 'My cousins went to school with them.' 'They looked normal enough.' Someone's brother is a policeman down in Christchurch and he says they've found the Pauline girl's diary. Someone says they're going to jail. Someone else says they'll be hospitalised. Everyone lowers their voices to talk about the other things the girls might have done together. They wonder if any of the girls they know are like that.

Diane's mother won't mention the murder. She throws the newspaper into the fire before Diane gets a chance to look. Every evening, she brushes Diane's hair so roughly that Diane thinks she's going to fall backwards. She stares hard at the mirror and fights to keep her eyes from watering. If she focuses, she can turn her mother's voice into radio static, but a few words cut through: *God, good, girl.*

If her mother finds out about Bruce, she'll be sent to her aunt's faster than she can pack a suitcase. She doesn't want to think about that. She wants to be back in the sand dunes, when it was warm enough to sneak out in her nightgown. She wants the scratch of a picnic rug underneath her. She wants to be inside her body and she wants Bruce there too. Her mother plaits her hair so tight Diane can feel the skin on her forehead being yanked back, then sends her to bed.

She lets the plaits out as soon as the door's shut, and gently rubs her scalp. She misses finding grains of sand under her fingertips.

—

Margaret's little sisters are whining, but if she shuts her bedroom door and turns the volume on her portable record player to full, she can almost ignore it. The record player is her most prized possession: a gift from her aunt, who lives in London now. It was her aunt who introduced her to Eartha Kitt, too. Margaret smokes a cigarette out her bedroom window to 'C'est si Bon' and tries to imagine she's in Paris, but her mother yells at her sisters to stay out of the kitchen and ruins the moment. Margaret doesn't want to be like her mother. When her mother was her age, she was already pregnant. Margaret's not going to have children: she's going to get a job in an office or a hotel and save up so she can move to Paris. Her teachers say she won't get school certificate at this rate, but she's top of French and her typing isn't bad.

The song finishes and for a moment all she can hear is the soft crackle of dust on the needle, then it's 'I Want to be Evil'. Margaret wiggles into her black skirt with the slit up the back and slips on the red heels that Rita gave her. They're a size too big, but if she puts a sock in the bottom they fit just right. The only make-up she owns is the lipstick stolen from the top drawer in her parents' ensuite—her mother never used it anyway. The tube is labelled 'Cherries in the Snow'. Cherry is *Cerise* in French. That's what Margaret's going to call herself when she moves to Paris.

Margaret tries to slip out the front door unnoticed, but before she can close it behind her she hears her mother from the kitchen.

'Tart.'

She hesitates for a moment. Her mother doesn't say anything else.

—

Rosemary's mother asks, 'Where's Caroline? Where's Caroline? Where's Caroline?', until Rosemary's afraid she could hit her. She digs out her best, high-necked sweater and cleans her saddle shoes. She tells her mother she's meeting friends at the Empress and promises she'll be home before ten.

On her way to the tram, she goes to the park and picks blackberries from the bush growing through the fence. She squeezes them until her hands are stained blood red. She pats the juice on her cheekbones like it's rouge, like Caroline taught her in summer, and washes off the rest in the drinking fountain. She can't get the red out of her heartline.

The Empress ballroom is all pastels and silver. There's a picture of the Queen hanging above the stage where the band is playing, and a nauseating cocktail of perfumes and cologne in the air. The boys line up on one side of the room and the girls line up on the other. They do the stroll, and all the ballroom steps Miss Dixon taught them, then pair off for slow dancing. The band plays 'If I Give My Heart to You', 'I'll See You in My Dreams', 'My Secret Love'. The girls pretend to look at the boy they're dancing with, but really they're looking over his shoulder, at everyone else in the room. They spot a hand reaching for a bum, then a foot getting stamped on. They spot a metal flask being slipped from pocket to pocket.

Rosemary dances with two boys she knows from the college next door, then finds herself dancing with one of the teddy boys she's seen hanging around Sunshine milk bar on the weekends. He's got a proper ducktail haircut and beetle crusher shoes and he's so tall her face barely reaches his lapels. She wonders if he knows she's only sixteen.

The longer they dance, the more certain she becomes that

she can smell someone's sweat. She's scared it's her own. When he lifts her arm to twirl her around, she sniffs her armpit. She can smell her deodorant through the wool. When he pulls her into his chest, the smell of sweat is overpowering. She tries not to breathe through her nose for the rest of the dance.

Rita picks up Margaret first, so she gets to sit up front. She clicks open the glovebox and finds a flashlight, a pink envelope of 'Durex Protectives' and half a packet of chewing gum. They both take a piece. Margaret crunches the sugary coating and chews it soft. Rita blows a bubble, then pops it with her tongue. Margaret can't help watching her. Rita's two years older: they only became friends because they were always in detention together. Now Rita works in a hotel and wears a uniform. She's the only girl who has a car. They make three more stops on the way to the dance hall, and arrive with four girls squished in the back, and one curled in the boot.

Boys flock to the car. They're all dressed like Marlon Brando in *The Wild One*: Levis and leather jackets, peaked train driver caps, flying boots with sheepskin along the top. One boy tries to put his arm around Rita but she shrugs him off and puts her arm around Margaret instead.

'In your dreams, joker.'

The music seems even louder than the week before and the room is full of colour: boys in blue suede shoes, bodgies with stovepipe trousers and hair so slick it reflects the light, girls in red slacks and gingham pedal pushers. Margaret dances with the usual crowd, and a few new faces. They jitterbug and jive. Someone sneaks in a bottle of gin and they take turns drinking it in the toilets. Margaret spots a boy wearing a black jacket with leopard-skin lining and points him out to Rita. She pushes Margaret towards him and soon he's lifting her into the air, twirling her in circles, whispering in her ear.

On the walk to the park, Margaret mentions she's cold and he puts his jacket over her shoulders. The park is too dark to see, but she can hear other couples: rustles, murmurs, a gasp. They find a spot under a tree and spread his jacket on the grass. It all happens faster than Margaret is used to. Just as it's starting to feel good, he pulls himself from her and liquid pools between her thighs. He zips himself back up and she looks at the stars. She wonders if anybody is watching.

When the dance is over, the teddy boy asks Rosemary if she wants to drive somewhere and she says, 'I guess.' His car's an old bomb, but she gets inside anyway. She asks to wind down a window, and when she smells the sea, she's relieved. She puts her head out and breathes in deep.

There's already a row of cars parked along Oriental Bay, and as he pulls up, she remembers Caroline saying this is where her cousin lost her virginity. The boy reaches an arm and slides her closer to him on the seat. Rosemary imagines telling all of this to Caroline. She can't decide whether she would call him a boy or a man. He parts her knees with his hand. She was careful when choosing her underwear to wear the ones with 'Friday' embroidered on them, but now it's past midnight and it's not Friday anymore, it's Saturday. This is all she can think about: Saturday, Saturday, Saturday.

When Rosemary gets home, her mother's waiting up for her in the kitchen. 'What happened?' she asks.

'I don't know,' Rosemary says. She knows her mother will think she's lying, but she isn't.

Diane leaves her window open. It's nearly midnight when she hears a joking whisper: '*Rapunzel, Rapunzel, let down your hair!*' It gives her such a fright she almost cries out and ruins the whole plan. Bruce climbs in and kisses her and it doesn't feel real: Bruce in her bedroom, her parents down the hall. The only light comes from the moon and stars outside. She's so excited and so terrified she's worried she'll faint and her mother will wake up at the sound.

They hurry out of their clothes and into her bed and Bruce is too tall to lie down properly and they want to laugh but they have to stay quiet. He kisses her jaw and her neck and she doesn't want him to stop, but if he leaves any kind of mark her mother will spot it. He reaches down for his jeans and takes one of the tiny envelopes from his pocket. She watches him put it on and she still can't believe it's really him, in her bed, where she has imagined him so many times. They try to move without making any sound, but right at the last moment, the bed frame shrieks and she loses her breath. Nobody hears.

Before Bruce goes, she asks him to leave something, so she doesn't wake up and wonder if it was a dream. He takes the notebook from her bedside table and writes three words in the back.

*

The postman knocks on the girls' front doors while they're eating their jam toast. His forehead is already damp with sweat, and his postbags are so heavy they're sliding off his shoulders. He has an envelope that won't fit in the mailbox. The girls thank him and take it. It's the size of a Little Golden picture book.

When their parents open the envelope, the booklet inside is plain grey with 'Report of the Special Committee on Moral

Delinquency in Children and Adolescents' printed in black letters. The girls' hearts speed up. It's the same feeling they get when they're called to the school office and can't think why: they're sure they've been caught doing something wrong. While their parents are in the bathroom, they skim the report's contents. *Homosexuality, carnal knowledge, teenage huntresses.*

When the girls get to school, they're quick to find other girls who got an envelope too. They whisper together about all the things they might be in trouble for: Did someone see them talking to the teddy boys on Courtenay Place? Did the neighbours hear them climbing out their bedroom window on Saturday night? Did their mother find their diary? Sometime during first period, they realise everyone got an envelope— even the old lady across the road, even the teachers.

They still can't work out what it means. Someone says it's the milk bar gang out in Lower Hutt. Boys and girls—even younger than they are—having orgies in picture theatres and living rooms. Their parents say the American movies are to blame. Their grandparents say it's the comic books. A lady on the radio says it's all because of the Coca-Cola and the milkshakes—especially the vanilla ones. They're laced with hypnotic sex stimulants, she tells the radio presenter. They're driving our teenagers mad.

Rosemary sits by the water fountain at lunch. She eats half the sandwich her mother packed, then feels sick and puts the rest back. She digs around in her satchel until she finds a penny. She throws it into the water and wishes harder than she's ever wished before.

Rosemary feels sick all through English. She excuses herself to the bathroom and sits on the toilet with her eyes closed, listening to other girls come and go. Finally, she lets herself out.

While Rosemary's rinsing her hands, Caroline comes out of the cubicle behind her. They stare at each other's reflections in the mirror. Caroline's eyes are red and puffy. She rushes out without washing her hands.

When Margaret gets home, her records have disappeared. She hurries outside to check the bin and finds her black skirt cut into pieces and her red shoes with the heels broken off. Tears blur her eyes as she picks through torn comic books and magazines to find her records, all snapped in half. A tear lands on the vinyl and slides across the grooves.

When her mother gets home from church group, Margaret storms into the kitchen ready to yell. Her mother is sitting at the kitchen table, her head in her hands. Margaret's mother only ever sits down to eat. When she sees Margaret in the doorway, she tells her she's not allowed to go out on weekends anymore, and she must come to church on Sundays. The exhaustion in her mother's face scares Margaret into silence.

She calls Rita on the phone that night. Even Rita sounds shaken. She tells her about the police roundup in Lower Hutt: one hundred and seven charges laid, six boys put on probation, five girls placed in state care. Two are girls Margaret used to dance with in the weekend. She wonders whether she'll ever see them again.

School assembly feels like a funeral. Diane can't focus on the prayers, but thinking about Bruce makes her anxious. Ever since the murders, her mother has talked more and more about sending her to her aunt's. She says the city is dangerous for young girls.

Miss Wilson tells the school that teachers will now be stationed at the gates every lunchtime, and reminds them that many girls go missing in Mount Victoria.

Diane sings 'River of No Return' inside her head. Bruce said once that Marilyn Monroe looked like Diane with her little white blouse and her hair all long like that. She's never paid attention to the lyrics before.

The radio stops playing all the girls' favourite songs. The only place they can listen to them is on the jukebox at the milk bar. They order drink after drink, just for an excuse to sit and listen. The dairy and the soda make their stomachs hurt, but it's better than going home.

A nineteen-year-old girl is shot dead in an Auckland milk bar. The girls' mothers warn them this is what can happen if you lead a boy on, and urge them to stay away from the milk bars and cafes. The papers describe the murderer as a 'spurned lover'. He'd ordered an orangeade only minutes before he fired the gun. The girls have to admit he's good-looking. He says he planned to fire a single shot into the ceiling: a stunt, meant to get her attention. When the police dragged him away, he was going to say, 'I'm not guilty—only guilty of being in love!' But the bullet hits her instead. When the police take him away, he's playing with a pot plant, pulling off pieces of green and throwing them into the air. He lapses into gibberish as soon as the milk bar or her name are mentioned.

Four months later, a twenty-year-old stabs a nineteen-year-old at a different Auckland milk bar, only a five-minute walk up the road. One of the girls has an older sister who was there when it happened. She tells them the younger boy had just put 'Earth Angel' on the jukebox. She can't listen to it anymore. Both of the milk-bar murderers are hanged at Mount Eden prison.

*

The boys stop dressing like Marlon Brando and start dressing like James Dean. *Rebel Without a Cause* is banned from theatres, but they've seen his red bomber jacket in the magazines. The girls go to *East of Eden* and cry in the dark.

No one sneaks out at lunch anymore. Instead, they sit above the rock garden that divides the boys' college from theirs. When they were in fourth form, they used to slide down the banks and talk to the boys, but now the fourth-formers all hang around at the top. One carves her name into an apple with her fingernail, then throws it at a group of boys down below. It hits one of them smack on the head. The girls laugh so hard they forget to look pretty. A teacher yells at them and they all jump. The girl who threw the apple is put in detention.

A woman from church sees Diane with Bruce and tells her mother. She gets to see Bruce only one more time before she's sent away. He tells her they'll get married, she's sixteen, but she shakes her head: they're under twenty-one, they need a guardian's consent. He promises he'll come find her and she promises she won't think of anything but him.

Margaret's period is late. With each day that passes, she finds it harder to breathe. It's like the air won't reach the bottom of her lungs anymore. In church, she's worried she'll pass out. The minister waves his hands in the air and yells about sin.

Paris feels further and further away.

At home, Margaret vomits in the toilet three mornings in a row. She turns round and her mother is watching from the doorway. She looks like she wants to be sick too.

On Rosemary's birthday, there's a brown paper parcel on the doorstep. She unwraps it in her bedroom and finds a music box painted cream with little pink flowers. There's a tiny gold key to open it, and the inside is lined with red velvet. It plays 'Greensleeves'—same as the ice-cream truck. The ballerina spins without a partner.

COTTAGEWHORES

I live in a yellow cottage with three beautiful women. We call ourselves the Haus of Hot Girl, the Princess Cottage, Cottagewhores. We have daisies, rosemary and lavender growing in our front garden. We have a trellis with wild roses climbing all over it: pink and red and yellow. We have a white stone fountain, with a nymph perched on the basin's edge. We're a two-minute walk from New World.

We get our periods at the same time—almost always on a full moon. We get pimples in the exact same spot. We take simultaneous naps in our separate bedrooms. We knock on each other's doors to check if anyone wants anything from the supermarket. We buy discounted lilies and roses, then hang the roses upside down to dry. We buy three punnets of strawberries before they're in season and agree that they're flavourless. We eat out of bowls that look like cabbage leaves.

I make us focaccia, with sliced vegetables and herbs arranged in floral patterns on top. I wrap cashew cheese in muslin cloth and leave it out to age. I soak blood-orange peels in jars of vodka. We joke that I'm both the mother and the man of the flat. When we find a wētā clinging to our

139

stone Virgin Mary, I'm the one who takes it outside.

We throw 'hoe-lloween' parties, pagan parties, poltergeist parties. We burn candles scented with sandalwood and pine. We hang four witch hats from the ceiling, suspended on invisible strings. We gather on the dance floor to sing, 'There's some whores in this house!' We stay up past the witching hour and into the crackhead hours. After we've had a nap, we order Uber Eats. The delivery guy knocks so hard the house shakes. We all get a fright. We crack into the fortune cookies before we eat our noodles and rice. The first one we open says, *You will have no problem in your home that you will not be able to solve.*

Our garden wall falls down—taking the front gate and the mailbox with it. The landlords say it'll be two months before they can get us a replacement. The grass in our front garden grows until it reaches our knees. When the landlords finally send someone to mow the lawn, he scalps it. Only a few patches of grass remain: the rest is dry and broken earth. When our friends come round, we warn them, *It's not a cottage anymore, it's a crackhouse.*

One flatmate gets her hours cut. One gets such bad leg cramps she can't walk. Two break up with their boyfriends. One gets rejected by both of her crushes in the space of a week. A favourite pair of undies go missing. We hear each other crying in our rooms. When we drag ourselves to the kitchen, we hear our flatmate singing 'Dream Baby Dream' in the bath.

We gather in the living room, under the heat pump. We tell each other about our dreams and our nightmares, and realise we all had a sex dream on the same night. We read out messages from our exes. One flatmate gets a text from the girl who rejected her last month, saying she's thought of a fun name for our flat: the thottage. We all ignore it. We tell each other stories about men asking us out, then pulling down their pants to show us their cancer scars when we say no. Men telling us we act different when we're around our friends. Men pinning us to the ground. We tell each other about the men we're sleeping with. We tell the men, *I live in a yellow cottage with three beautiful women.*

GHOST STORY

The first playlist I made after meeting you was private. I called it *SEANCE PARTY*, so it wouldn't look conspicuous to the friends who scrolled through Spotify on my phone.

The event name had been 'Paranormal Partytime'. Around fifteen guests took part in the seance itself—most people were downstairs drinking and dancing. No alcohol was allowed into the seance room. 'Season of the Witch' drifted up through the floorboards.

The girl who was running the seance was taking it all very seriously. Her name was Willow, though I felt confident this hadn't been her birth name. First, she sprayed everyone's hands with Mario Badescu toner. 'Cleansing water,' she said, 'to rid your bodies of any negative energy you're bringing into the space.'

I scanned the other faces in the room to see if anyone else found this funny. You raised your eyebrows and smiled at me.

Willow told us to sit in a circle. You and I sat next to each other, though I wasn't sure whether this was intentional on your part. She told us all to hold hands. Your fingers slid cool into mine.

When everyone was settled, Willow said a prayer to protect us from harm and to open the seance. She took a crystal pendant from a velvet bag and held it in the air. She began swinging it from side to side.

'Are there any spirits who would like to speak?'

The pendant kept swinging.

She moved her finger just enough that it began swinging in another direction. I grinned into my lap.

'Yes, great. Are you a male?'

The pendant kept swinging in the affirmative. Your fingers moved in my hand.

'Awesome. Now, did you enter the spirit realm in the last century? Yup? The last ninety years?'

This line of questioning continued down to sixty years. I glanced at you. Your eyes were focused on the carpet. Most other people in the circle had their eyes closed. You and I were the only ones smiling.

'Did you die of natural causes?'

The pendant began swinging in a slightly different direction. Willow gasped.

'Were you . . . murdered?'

The pendant confirmed.

'Were you killed in this room?'

Another yes. You were trying not to laugh. I looked away quickly.

'Were you killed—' Willow stopped when she realised another girl in the circle was close to tears. I heard you choke out a giggle, then cover it up with a loud cough. I bit down hard on my lip, but a squeak of laughter escaped. You squeezed my hand.

Just as actual tears started running down the girl's face, a chorus of voices from downstairs yelled, 'PSYCHO KILLER! QU'EST-CE QUE C'EST!' My body trembled with the effort of not laughing as a low rumble of 'fa-fa-fa-fa better' sounded beneath us. I tried to ignore the muffled giggles coming from you.

She was really sobbing now. The girls on either side of her had their arms around her shoulders and were asking if she was okay. Downstairs, everyone was joining in on the 'Ay-ya-ya-ya-ya-ya'. I tried to control my breathing.

'I think we should wrap up now,' Willow said, hurrying the pendant back into its little bag.

Everyone let go of each other's hands. You and I were already getting up to leave as she thanked the spirits for joining us and wished them on their way. We burst out of the room and cracked up all the way down the stairs—only catching our breath as we stepped back into the party. 'Nights in White Satin' was playing, and a group of girls were dancing with their arms around each other. I threw my hands out and spun in a slow circle. You watched.

We found our drinks. When the theme from *Suspiria* played, I asked whether you'd seen it. We discussed the remake versus the original, then we were talking about music.

'I should add you on Spotify.' You typed in my name and hit 'follow'. I felt the same rush as when you had squeezed my hand in the seance. You scrolled briefly through my public playlists.

I folded my arms. 'Are you one of those Spotify desktop people who watches what everyone's listening to?'

Your eyes locked on mine. 'Sometimes, yeah. I keep my listening activity hidden, though.'

'Are you into musical theatre or something?'

You laughed. 'No. I'm just a private person.'

Since we'd come downstairs, you kept giving me this mysterious smile, like you knew something I didn't. It seemed rehearsed, picked up from movies. This didn't stop me from liking it.

Nina Simone's 'I Put a Spell on You' began to play, and someone turned out the lights. The room was lit only by the candles on the mantelpiece. I watched your lips move as you were speaking, but really I was listening to the music. You asked me a question.

'Huh?'

'Do you believe some people are supposed to meet?'

I held your gaze, determined not to show any embarrassment. 'You mean like fate?'

You nodded and sipped your drink.

'I guess so, yeah. Do you?'

'I'm not sure yet.'

'Blue Monday' came on, and we put down our drinks to dance. We didn't break eye contact for the whole song.

Everyone danced together for 'Murder on the Dancefloor'. A group of girls came in from outside. One of them touched your arm and whispered something in your ear. You nodded and kissed her cheek.

'We're heading off,' you said.

parallel universe

There weren't many public playlists on your Spotify profile, and they didn't have cover photos or descriptions like mine. I searched you up on Facebook and Instagram. Nothing. All I found on Google was an empty Pinterest account and a series of death notices from 2015 for someone with the same name.

I looked at who you followed on Spotify: all my favourite artists, a bunch of accounts with a long number for a username, a couple of people I recognised. I checked their Instagram accounts for pictures of you. No luck.

I scrolled through the seance party invite list and clicked on all the girls I didn't know until I found the one you had left with. Her name was Clara. Most of her Facebook photos were private, but I found one of you together on her Instagram, posted a month ago. I typed her username into an anonymous Instagram story viewer and watched a video she had put up that morning: a bee buzzing around a lavender bush.

I checked again the next day. Her username popped up as soon as I typed a 'c'. You were on my screen. I felt shocked, despite this being exactly what I was checking for. The clip had no sound. You were in track pants and a Mazzy Star T-shirt, and you were shaking a Magic 8 ball. The camera zoomed in on the blue triangle as it settled on an answer. *Cannot predict now.*

I didn't check your Spotify account, or Clara's Instagram, for a few weeks after that. I was scrolling through my own Instagram profile, half-asleep, when a notification came through inviting me to a party at Willow's house. I checked the guest list. Clara was on it. I hit 'maybe' and put my phone face down on the bed.

I picked it up again seconds later, opened Spotify and typed in your name. A new playlist had been made public. I felt very awake now. The first song was 'Femme Fatale'. I wondered whether you thought of yourself as a femme fatale, or someone else. I stopped when I got to 'Next Lifetime'. My friend Kate had listened to this song on repeat for a few months in high school, when she thought she was in love with a boy who wasn't her boyfriend. By the chorus, I was back in Kate's car—McDonald's wrappers all over the floor, both of us chewing watermelon gum and singing about wanting a person we couldn't have.

My heart beat hard. I kept scrolling.

When I got to 'Blue Monday' I heard myself say 'No fucking way' to my empty bedroom.

SHOOT YOUR SHOT

I made a new playlist immediately. I put 'Pussy is God' near the top, in case you were under the impression I was straight, and uploaded a cover picture I'd found on Instagram of a cake in a heart shape, with 'SO HOT YOU'RE HURTING MY FEELINGS' written on it.

I listened to the playlist at full volume while I was getting ready for Willow's party. I mouthed 'I Wanna Be Your Lover' to the mirror. I hummed along to 'Le Temps De L'amour' while trimming my nails. I knew nothing could really happen between us while you were still seeing Clara, but if I made it obvious I was interested in you too, it seemed possible you would break up with her—or at the very least open things up. You'd added 'Jupiter 4' to the *parallel universe* playlist just the other day.

My Bluetooth speaker started beeping a low battery alert while I was trying on clothes, then died while I was zipping up my boots. The house was uncomfortably quiet. I plugged the speaker in to charge and ordered an Uber.

Kate Bush came on the radio just after I got in, singing 'Hounds of Love'. The driver turned it off halfway through the song—leaving us in dead silence. He made no attempt at conversation, and all the questions I thought of were so boring that I stayed quiet too. The car was muggy and smelled of fresh leather.

It was a relief to escape into the noise of the party. I did a quick scan of the room but couldn't see you. Maybe you weren't here. I had no way of contacting you. If you didn't come tonight, how would I see you again? I weaved through the crowd and into the hall, checking all the rooms. The first was clearly Willow's parents', and the second had bunk beds in it, but I could smell incense drifting from the third room. When I nudged the door, Willow and a bunch of boys came into view.

'Hey!' Willow noticed me in the doorway. Her hands were hovering over one of the boys' legs, like she was giving him reiki. 'Did you get the ladder up to the attic?'

'Nah, I'm just leaving—'

'Weren't you one of the people trying to climb into the attic? With that other girl, Clara's ex?'

The word reverberated through my body. 'Where's the ladder again?'

towers in the attic

A wooden ladder had been unfolded from a square hole in the laundry's ceiling, but it didn't reach all the way to the ground. Up above, I could hear music playing off a tinny speaker and some muffled conversation. I climbed onto the washing machine and up the ladder. Three faces spun towards me. One of them was yours.

'You're here!' You hurried over to help me up. Once I was standing, you hugged me. You were wearing the same pants you'd worn to the seance party, but this time they had a drink stain across the thigh.

'What are you doing up here?'

'She's hiding in case Clara turns up,' said the other girl. I could see how Willow had mistaken me for her—we had a similar haircut, and were both wearing corset-style tops. She was sitting on the floor next to a guy I'd seen on Instagram: his hair dyed bright blue. There was a set of tarot cards laid out in front of them, along with two wine bottles and three plastic cups.

'Want a tarot reading?' You were doing the mystery smile, but the alcohol had loosened it into something closer to a genuine grin.

'Sure.' I sat down next to the girl on the floor while she shuffled the cards back into a deck. It was darker up here than downstairs, but the trapdoor let in a soft glow. Most of the light came from two large torches, switched on and positioned to either side of the Bluetooth speaker. We were surrounded by stacks of cardboard boxes labelled 'SEWING' and 'EM'S KITCHEN'. There was an old rocking horse pushed into the corner, and Pink Batts fitted between the wooden slats in the ceiling. I rubbed my arms. It was cold.

'Here, share with me.' You refilled your cup with red wine.

I thanked you and gulped it down.

You fished a tiny booklet out of the tarot box. 'Is just three cards okay? We've been making it up as we go.'

'Three's good.'

I picked the cards out and you laid them face down on the floor. Swells of ASMR moved down the back of my neck to my spine and shoulders.

'I need you to think of a question you want to ask, or a situation you want to focus on.'

You were staring at me.

I stared back. 'I've got one.'

'Okay. The first card represents your past, in relation to whatever you've got in mind.'

I turned over the same card pictured on the box: 'The Magician'.

You read from the booklet. 'This is a powerful card. The Magician represents manifestation: using willpower to get what you desire. Your dreams and your reality are only reflections of one another.'

The other two laughed, but you looked at me with genuine interest. 'Do you believe that?'

After a pause, I nodded. 'I'm not sure how good at manifesting I am, though. I just obsess.'

Before I could ask if you believed too, the girl next to me cut in.

'Next one.'

I could feel the wine warming my body. I refilled the cup we were sharing and took another sip.

You pointed your finger at the middle card. 'This is your present situation.'

I flipped it over. Flames, lightning, falling bodies.

'Ha,' you said. 'I got this one for my past. It's the worst card.'

'So it was obviously about Clara and the break up,' the girl next to me added.

You paged through the booklet again. 'The Tower represents upheaval and disaster. A strong structure built on shaky ground, knocked down by a single bolt of lightning. Expect the unexpected.'

'Wow, that's helpful,' I said.

'Maybe the last one will be better,' you said.

The only card I could think of was the heart with three swords stabbed into it. I turned over the future. No swords, no heart.

'The Wheel of Fortune is a symbol of inevitable cycles: it reminds you to make the most of the blissful moments in your life, for soon they could be gone. Outside forces are influencing your situation. You cannot always be in control.'

I frowned. 'That could mean anything.'

The girl shrugged. 'Any of it could mean anything.'

You gathered up the cards and slotted them back into their box, along with the booklet. A chill passed through the room.

'Where did that come from?' said the girl.

You smirked. 'Maybe it's a ghost.'

Something slammed and the girl screamed, startling my body into a little jump.

'Jesus Christ, woman,' the boy said, pressing his hand to his heart.

You appeared unbothered by both the slam and the scream. 'That thing was teetering all night.' You nodded at the fallen banana box—spilling faded *National Geographic*s to the floor.

The boy shook out his arms, then held up a joint between his middle and index fingers. 'Do you reckon I can smoke up here?'

'Nah, there's no windows,' you said. 'The smell will stick.'

'All right, I'm heading out then. Any of you want to join?'

The girl nodded. I looked at you. You smiled at me and didn't say anything.

'See ya,' they said, climbing back down the ladder. We heard them thump onto the floor, then the boy's voice again, softer, but not soft enough. 'She's moving on fast.'

There was a hissing sound, then he yelled out an 'Ow!'

Your cheeks were as pink as mine. 'Shut Up Kiss Me' began to play.

DREAMING

I was curious to see your bedroom, but you said it was too messy. We Ubered to mine. You sat on my bed with your hands in your lap while I fussed around with curtains and lamps. I wasn't sure whether to put on music. I'd had one girlfriend who hated music during sex, and a few boyfriends who found it distracting. I could put on an album, but it might end at an awkward time. If I'd thought the night would turn out like this I would have prepared a playlist. I scrolled through my recently played and hit shuffle on *ROAD TRIP*. It was eight hours long, so at least it wouldn't cut off.

We made out for the first few songs, then sometime during 'Biscuit', I asked to undo your belt. From there, the songs blurred together. I remember you telling me I smelled good during 'How's That'. I remember taking your top off just as 'Space Song' started to play, and realising I owned the red version of your white bra. I remember going down on you at the start of 'Anemone'. I remember kissing the insides of your thighs in the silence between songs. I remember you pulling my hair during 'Dissolved Girl'. I remember 'Don't Cha' coming on and trying to ignore it, then apologising and reaching for my phone to press 'skip'. I remember the bed squeaking at the end of 'Jigsaw Falling Into Place'. I remember getting my vibrator out of my drawer during 'New Love Cassette', and you saying you were too drunk to come. I don't remember what song was playing when I came.

It started raining afterwards. I turned off the music and opened the window so we could listen. The night air made my entire body goosebump. We huddled under my duvet.

'Did you know this was going to happen?' I asked.

'I hoped it might.'

'In a parallel universe?'

You cringed and covered your face. I laughed until you peeled your hands away.

'So . . .' I pulled at a loose thread on my duvet cover. 'When exactly did you and Clara break up?'

I kept my eyes on the duvet, though I wished I could see your reaction.

You hesitated before speaking. 'I ended things about a week ago.' You said this slowly, like you were still thinking about it. 'I should have done it earlier.'

I glanced up. Your eyes were focused on your fingernails.

'Is Clara going to hate me?' A part of me hoped the answer would be yes. I liked feeling that I had something Clara should be jealous of.

'No . . .' You looked at me. 'I mean, she's not confrontational or anything.'

I smiled. 'Don't worry, I'm not stressed about it.'

You smiled too, then ran your hand down my arm. 'You're such a chill person.'

I laughed. 'I'm glad I come across that way.'

You drifted off not long after that. I always found it hard to sleep with a new person in my bed, but I didn't mind lying awake next to you. Your leg twitched, then your arm. I wondered what you were dreaming about.

I spent every spare moment in the days that followed reliving that night in my mind. I replayed every tiny memory so many times I began to wonder if the effect would wear off. I knew there were studies that proved your memories changed every time you re-remembered them, but I felt certain I was remembering these ones right.

Even more memories came back to me when I listened to

the *ROAD TRIP* playlist. I added some of these songs to the
playlist I had made for dreaming up future nights with you.
Sometimes I worried that by imagining these things in such
detail, I would prevent them from ever happening. I talked to
you about this the next time we slept together.

It was the first time I'd been to your house. Your room was
mostly how I thought it would be: records and a dusty record
player, plants in the windowsill, overflowing laundry basket.
The only things I hadn't expected were your black bedsheets,
black duvet cover and black pillow cases. I shuffled the pillow
under my head.

'Do you believe that once you imagine something a
certain way, it can never happen exactly how you imagined
it?' I asked. 'Like, by thinking it you make it impossible?'

'Give me an example.'

'I don't know. Like, if I imagined you putting your hand
on my thigh and kissing my neck it could never happen like
it did in my mind.'

You put your hand on my thigh and kissed my neck.

'No, the way I imagined it was spontaneous. You're proving
my point!'

'I don't dream that much.' You were doing the mystery
smile again.

I rolled my eyes. 'Sure, sure.'

Your mouth opened, then shut. You looked at your
fingernails. 'I guess I've only ever thought about it with bad
things.'

'What do you mean?'

You clenched your hand into a fist, then flexed your
fingers. 'When I was little I thought that if you imagined all
the bad things that could happen to you, it might stop them
from happening.' You chewed your index fingernail. 'I was

kind of obsessive about it. I used to lie in bed trying to think of all the ways my parents could die. Stuff like that.'

I squeezed your arm. 'That's so sad!'

You shrugged. 'But now I sometimes feel like if you imagine a bad thing happening, it's an omen. Or a premonition.'

I waited for you to go on.

You ran your hands through your hair. 'When me and my ex broke up—'

'Clara?'

'No. He was a guy. After we broke up, I remember I saw some joke online about the bisexual struggle of watching the guy you like start dating the girl you like. As soon as I read that, I imagined my ex on a date with this one girl I had a crush on, even though they didn't know each other or anything. Then like two weeks later, I see them together at a gig.'

'Maybe you manifested it.'

'Maybe.'

You rolled on your side so we were facing each other. 'I don't think I've ever told anyone any of that before.'

The look on your face made me believe you. There was no trace of a mystery smile.

While you had a shower, I flicked through the copy of *Picnic at Hanging Rock* on your bedside table. Some sentences were underlined, and there was a dried flower tucked between two of the pages. You must have read it before. On the front, there was a black and white picture of a girl lying on the ground, sleeping.

I opened up the title page. Everything froze. Clara's name was written in the cover. Her handwriting was a neat cursive—nothing like my left-handed scrawl. I shut the book and tried to put it back in the same position, but couldn't remember how I'd found it. The sound of the shower running continued through the walls. I pushed the book to the other side of the table and put the water bottle in its place, as if I'd moved the book so it wouldn't get wet.

I unplugged my phone from your charger. The last time I'd looked at Clara's Instagram was before the attic party— she didn't even pop up in my recent searches. I typed in her full username. No results. My breath quickened. Maybe she'd deleted her profile. Maybe she'd changed her handle. I switched to my ghost account and entered her name again. She came up right away.

'Hey.'

My body jolted like I'd tripped over in a dream. I hadn't noticed the shower turning off, or the door opening. Now you were standing right in front of me in a grey towel, dripping water on the carpet. Your skin was red and blotchy from the heat of the shower.

'What's up?'

I ummed for a moment, but couldn't see any point in lying. 'Clara blocked me.'

Your eyebrows shot up. 'Really? That was quick.'

You got a T-shirt out of your drawer. I could see your reflection in the mirror—smiling slightly.

I hesitated. 'What happened with you two?'

You pulled the T-shirt over your head. 'We were too different. She's a really serious person.'

I sat up in bed. 'Do you reckon we're different?'

You lifted one arm, then the other, to put on deodorant. 'I think we're similar. You're more like me than Clara.'

'How so?'

'I don't know. We find the same things funny, we like

female manipulator music, we're both kind of slutty . . .'

'You just described half the people we know.'

You sat down next to me on the bed. 'I just feel like we got each other right away, even at the seance party.'

I nodded. 'I felt that too.'

Soundtrack

I waited until we'd been sleeping together for a month before I suggested we make each other a playlist. You said we should start a collaborative one instead.

I titled it and uploaded a cover photo of two girls wearing sheer blue veils, their faces mostly disguised. The first song I added was 'True Love Waits', because of the line about haunted attics. You teased me for starting off with something so depressing.

'212' was when we took caps at that party. I kept apologising for talking so much and you kept laughing and saying it was nice. We chewed on peppermint gum. You pointed out a girl you'd dated and a guy you'd slept with and I tried not to feel jealous, even though I'd had a thing with one of the hosts a couple of years back.

Willow asked if we were together and we grinned but didn't answer. 'I remember you two giving each other the eyes during the seance,' she said. 'I knew you'd end up dating.'

We danced together for the first time since the seance party. I made MDMA-fuelled confessions about monogamy and the future and my feelings for you. You kissed me and promised it was all going to be good.

I woke up anxious that I'd said too much. I tried to

DREAM GIRL

remember exactly what your responses had been, but all I could think of was you smiling under the disco lights.

'Blue Flower' was a Tuesday. You'd come to mine after your shift with leftover cannelloni and tiramisu. We ate them on my bed, then abandoned the plastic containers to take off each other's clothes. Our bodies cast shadows on my sloped ceiling. We looked like a movie.

We ran a bath afterwards. I poured in too much lavender oil and the smell was overwhelming, but you insisted it was fine. We stared at each other for a long time from our opposite ends of the tub.

You said, 'I feel like you can see right through me.'

I was pleased, but really I felt like I was still getting to know you.

'Nightcall' was when you were two hours later than you'd said you'd be. I was in a bad mood when you arrived. You apologised, then tried to turn it into a joke, which pissed me off more. You asked if you should leave, and for a second you looked like you might cry.

We fucked and felt better. In the dark, we listed off things we liked about each other. You liked that I could go with the flow, I was a careful listener, my room always smelled nice. I thought you were a better listener than me, and I liked that you had a good memory and always brought me food. At one point, I slipped and almost said love. You squeezed my hand.

'Under Your Spell' was when you started working night shifts. You warned me you might not be able to hang out as much and I said that was okay, though I secretly hoped it wouldn't be true. Every second night dropped to two nights a week, then one. You were too tired to have sex. We slept facing away from each other.

I sent a text the next day asking how you were going. You replied a few hours later saying you were okay, but didn't reply when I asked if you were free later in the week. I waited until the evening to call you. No answer. I texted again. No answer. I called, I called, I called. No answer.

I tried to give you space, but couldn't help texting and calling the next day, and the one after that. By the end of the week, my fear that you were ignoring me morphed into fear that something had happened to you. I imagined you hit by a car, then remembered what you had said about omens and tried to block the thought from my mind. Eventually I gave in and messaged your flatmate. You were in your room.

I added 'Lover, You Should've Come Over' to the playlist, hoping you would add something in response. I didn't hear from you for ten days. I thought about turning up at your house, your work, but didn't want to seem crazy. You didn't add any songs to the playlist. I added 'You Keep Me Hangin' On'. 'How Come U Don't Call Me Anymore?' 'Anyone's Ghost.'

GIVE UP THE GHOST

The first song was 'So Sad So Sexy'. I wanted you to know I was heartbroken, but also thriving. I put 'Music to Watch Boys To' and 'More Women' near the top, too. I listened to this part of the playlist in the daytime, when I was out doing things. I listened to the second part of the playlist when I was alone in my room. I played 'Watching You Without Me' on repeat.

I imagined you alone in your room, too: watching movies

on your laptop, taking a hot-water bottle to bed. I imagined you in your room with someone else: a faceless girl, a blurred copy of Clara. I read diary entries from when we first met while Angie Stone sang 'Wish I Didn't Miss You'.

It wasn't the obvious memories that made me miss you, like kissing in the attic, or waking up with you in my bed. It was the tiny, unexpected ones. It was watching you from my window—crossing the road with a paper bag of fresh-picked basil in your hand. How you ran your hands through your hair when you were nervous or embarrassed. Finding a painting in an old art history book of a girl who looked so much like you that I claimed she was your past self. The grin on your face when I insisted on playing you 'Teardrops'. I'd made a fist in front of my mouth, like I was gripping a microphone, and held my other hand up to your face to stop you speaking over the lyrics. 'Wait—wait for the bridge.'

When the invite for 'The Haunting of 42 Cain Street' came through, I hit 'going' without even checking the date. 42 Cain Street was where the seance party had been. The thought of seeing you again made me nervous to the point of light-headedness, and also filled me with a sense of dread, but there was no way I was going to pass it up.

Getting ready gave me déjà vu. No matter how many times I told myself there was no chance you and I would end up hooking up again tonight, I still wondered if we would. I could hardly believe the coincidence when I got in the Uber and Kate Bush was playing. It was 'Cloudbusting'. I sang along to the chorus.

The driver grinned at me in the rear-view mirror. 'Should I turn it up?'

'All right.'

I watched the time on the car radio. It was nearly 1am. This was later than usual for me, but I'd known there was a chance you'd work a night shift and wouldn't get to the party until midnight. I wanted to arrive after you did.

I thanked the driver as I got out. The street was quieter than I expected. All I could hear from the house was a low rumble of people talking. No music.

The Uber drove away and I dug my perfume out of my bag. There was another girl whispering into her phone further down the street, but it was too dark to tell if I knew her. I sprayed perfume into the ends of my hair and scrunched it with my hands. I wondered if you would smell me before you saw me.

When I heard your laugh, I froze. It sounded like you were floating above my head. I looked up and saw you standing on the balcony, talking to someone in a puffer jacket. You were wearing the white jumper you'd lent me every time I forgot to bring a long sleeve to yours. I couldn't hear what you were saying.

The other person handed you their vape, and you sucked on it. The wind blew the clouds of vapour over your shoulder and your hair across your face. I wished you'd turn round so I could see you properly, but I didn't want you to spot me down here on my own. What if you and this person were hooking up?

You handed back the vape and pointed up at the moon. It was awkwardly close to being full—as if it had been drawn by someone who was bad at circles.

'Hey, sorry, do you have a lighter?'

My eyes snapped back to the street. The girl who'd been on the phone was now only a couple metres in front of me.

She stepped closer, then stopped. 'Oh shit. It's you.'

I stared at her. Clara.

'Oh.' I tried to think of something to say, but I was stuck. She was smaller than I remembered: without heels, she was shorter than me. Her hair looked freshly cut and styled.

She pointed her unlit cigarette at the house. 'She's not in there.'

'Who?'

'Who do you think?'

I frowned. 'She's literally right up there.' I pointed at the balcony. It was empty.

Clara didn't even look up. 'Trust me, she's not. It's her brother's twenty-first tonight. She's down south.'

My body tensed, my bag strap tight in my fist.

Clara raised her eyebrows. 'So she ghosted you too, hey?'

I swallowed my surprise. 'How do you know that?'

Clara laughed. 'I saw your Spotify.'

My mouth fell open, then I laughed as well. 'Shit.'

We kept laughing. Clara stuffed her cigarette back in its pack.

I cleared my throat. 'I'm sorry if I . . .'

She shrugged. 'It's not your fault. She would have found someone else if it wasn't you. I thought she was going to hook up with that other chick who went up to the attic. Your doppelganger.'

'We don't look that similar.'

Clara didn't seem to hear. She looked up at the moon and blinked a few times. 'Do you know she broke up with me over text? Then stopped messaging completely. I haven't heard a word since. She still hasn't given my books back.' She hugged her coat closer to her body. 'I should have known it would happen. She was seeing another girl when I met her, too. I must have believed I was too special for it to happen to me, or something. Or that we were meant to be together. Seems insane now.'

We stood in silence for a moment. I thought about what I'd seen on the balcony, but when I tried to imagine your face, clouds of vapour got in the way.

I coughed. 'So, why's there no music at the party?'

'Noise control took the speakers.'

halley's comet

I continued to check your Spotify profile regularly. It had been more than two months since I'd last seen you when you posted the *halley's comet* playlist. I felt sure the title was supposed to mean something, but I had no idea what. I skimmed the Wikipedia page, and highlighted some lines explaining that it's possible to see Halley's Comet twice in a lifetime. It last appeared in 1986, which was a decade before either of us was born.

Maybe the title was an inside joke between you and someone new. Maybe her name was Halley. The songs weren't especially romantic—I couldn't imagine putting 'Climbing Up the Walls' or 'Dream Brother' on a crush playlist. A lot of the artists were unfamiliar to me.

You must have known that I would see it. If the playlist was really only meant for one person, you would have set it to private, and sent it to them individually. I scrolled to the bottom. The last track was 'The Party' by St Vincent. Which party were you thinking of?

I checked your profile again the next day to see if you'd added any new songs. The playlist was gone. You mustn't have meant to make it public in the first place.

NIGHTMARE GIRL

I love a girl, but she is so sour. The only foods she likes are in the citrus family. If she could take a pill instead of eating, she would. She drinks rotten milk and spends the night vomiting instead of coming to my house to eat the dinner I made for her. She is always cancelling on me, and often takes more than a day to reply. She blames this on being a Gemini. She says she doesn't need other people: she's an introvert, she's happiest alone. She calls herself curious, but easily distracted. She says her bite is bigger than her bark.

When she comes over, we play Truth. I'm never sure how much I should believe. She tells me love is just a chemical reaction. She thinks it's more mature to live in your fears than your fantasies. She doesn't believe in feelings, only logic. She's never remembered any of her dreams. She calls them silly things.

I go back through my journals and find an entry from months earlier. *We talked about lucid dreams (we both get the awareness, not much control), and the feeling of waking up from a dream and trying to fall back into it. She told me about her flying dreams, and was surprised that I never have them.*

I flick back a few more months.

She tells me that her favourite grandmother never remembers any dreams. 'Silly things,' her grandmother calls them.

The girl I love calls me unattainably hot, but I have made myself so attainable to her. She says, It's not that I do like you or don't like you. She just wants to be friends for now: wait and see. We make out on my bed.

The next day, she tells our friends she made a kiss-take. She tells them I said that I want to be heartbroken.

She comes over again. We talk on my bed. She tells me I'm her backup backup backup. She says she's attracted to people who have an elegant way of thinking, and I have that. I tell her I know. She says exactly. I look at her. You don't like me because I like myself? She nods. I point out that she hasn't said sorry and she says do I have to?

In my dreams, the girl I love makes out with my best friend at my birthday party, then tries to convince me it wasn't her; it was her sister. She kisses me and my teeth all crumble into her mouth. We play Two Truths and a Lie and she says, I never liked you, I never liked you, I never liked you.

PETS

Wallace loved Bartholomew in a way they didn't love anybody else. Their voice was different when they talked about him.

'There are only ten other Hermann's tortoises in the whole country.' Wallace ran their finger along Bartholomew's bumpy shell as he crept across the carpet. We were sitting in a circle with Bartholomew in the middle—like kids playing Show and Tell. Wallace told us they were given baby Bartholomew for their fifth birthday by their parents' hippy friend, Magnolia. 'Mum was so mad, she tried to get rid of him.'

Bartholomew lived outside in a clamshell-shaped paddling pool half-filled with soil, but Wallace brought him in to crawl around the living-room floor whenever they were home. He could usually be found under the dining table, chewing on a crinkled piece of kale, or some raw broccoli. In Wallace's desk drawer there was a handwritten contract signed by their sister, saying she would care for Bartholomew if Wallace died in a freak accident.

'He'll probably live longer than I do.' Wallace patted his head with the pad of their finger. 'He could be as long as a ruler by then.'

Bartholomew featured regularly on Wallace's Instagram

account, and all of our friends' accounts too. We loved to balance an object on his shell and video him walking around with it: a tube of Pringles, a toy Sylvanian, a mooncup. We were always saying we wished we had pets as cool as Bartholomew, but it wasn't until Estelle that anyone did anything about this. When Estelle fixated on something, she had to have it. We called this 'Veruca Salt energy'. Within a month of Estelle meeting Bartholomew, she had two pet chinchillas.

'This is Chin,' she said, pointing to the black chinchilla. It hopped away from her finger, towards its cream-coloured friend. 'And this is Chilla. Like in the Nabokov story.'

None of us had read any Nabokov story, but this was typical Estelle. She gave us a mini box of raisins to feed Chin and Chilla, and we took turns letting them nibble the tiny dried fruit from between our finger and thumb. Estelle left the room and came back carrying two large bowls, and an orange canister labelled 'VOLCANIC DUST'. Estelle poured the sandy powder into the bowls, then placed Chin and Chilla inside. We watched them flip around, sending puffs of dust into the air.

'They can't get wet, because their fur is so dense,' Estelle told us. 'They'd be freezing to death by the time the water dried.'

The chinchillas were unbelievably soft, but when you got too close, they looked like rats. They didn't smell like rats. Their fur seemed to have absorbed the smell of Estelle's bedroom: pomegranate diffuser oil and Diptyque perfume.

'Are they boys or girls?' we asked.

'Definitely girls.'

Next came Chloe and the Bengal. Even Katy, who didn't like cats, had to admit this kitten was beautiful. It was as if someone had taken a leopard and shrunk it down to the smallest possible size. He looked like he belonged in a tropical rainforest, or a bushy savannah: far too exotic to be leaping around Chloe's flat.

'It's like he's wearing eyeliner.' Katy peered at the little black wings in the outer corners of his eyes.

Chloe scooped him into her arms and kissed the spot between his ears. 'I'm calling him Bagel. Bagel the Bengal.'

We nodded. Naming the pets was half the fun. A good name could upgrade a pet from cool to really cool.

'Was he expensive?'

Chloe raised her eyebrows in a way that meant yes. 'And silver Bengals are double the price.'

'You can get silver ones?'

'You can get all sorts.' Chloe sat down, and Bagel curled into a bagel-shape on her lap. 'Snow Bengals, Blue Bengals . . . the Snow Lynx Bengals are super gorgeous. They have blue eyes their whole life. Their fur is, like, cream-coloured, with golden spots. The silver ones look like snow leopards.'

'Did you tell your landlady about him?'

Chloe shook her head. 'She'd say no. I'm just going to put him in the car when we have inspection.'

'What if she turns up unexpected?'

'I'll say he wandered in off the street.'

As soon as we heard Katy had got a chameleon, we all messaged asking to come over. The group chat debated what she should call the chameleon (gender unknown), until Katy settled on Roy, short for ROYGBIV.

'How do you make it change colour?' Chloe asked, holding Roy's green body up to her pink sleeve.

'It can only turn brown or black,' Katy said.

'Oh.' Disappointment rippled through the room.

Katy moved Roy onto her own sleeve, which was dark grey. We watched its skin speckle brown, then shift into a mottled grey-black.

'Whoa,' we all said. We said this again when Roy's long and pink tongue shot out. It was at least half the length of Roy's whole body, and looked more like an intestine than a tongue.

We were having cocktails at Wallace's house when Lea posted the pictures. Bartholomew was under Wallace's chair, eating a slice of mango very, very slowly, while the rest of us drank margaritas very, very quickly. Our phones were all face up on the table, and whenever one of us got a notification, we would end up checking Instagram too. It was Estelle who saw the post first.

'You're fucking kidding me.'

We swarmed around the phone. Lea was semi-nude in the photos, but nothing reportable could be seen. Twisting around Lea's neck and chest was a bright green snake. She held its smooth head delicately in one hand, and a red apple in the other. The caption read 'Meet Medusa', followed by the snake emoji.

'Dumb name,' we all agreed. 'Too predictable.'

'A fucking apple.' Estelle was seething.

On Lea's Instagram story there were videos of Medusa wriggling in her bedsheets, then of Lea in a bra with Medusa winding knots around her fingers. Suddenly our videos of Bartholomew carrying around sanitary products seemed childlike, embarrassing. Medusa's skinny red tongue flicked across Lea's boob.

'Look!' Estelle tapped the screen so the clip played again.

When we looked closely, we could see the tongue's fork. Estelle played it over and over.

'How did she get that into the country?' Wallace was looking at the photos on their own phone now. 'Snakes are illegal here.'

'And where are the videos of her feeding it?' Chloe asked. 'Snakes are carnivores. She'll totally have to feed it bugs and worms and stuff. Maybe even mice.'

'True, they sell big bags of them in America. "Arctic Mice". You buy them frozen.'

We all grimaced. No pet could be worth frozen mice.

Lea's pictures meant game on. Estelle threw a chinchilla picnic. In the photos, Chin and Chilla crouched on a gingham blanket—eating rosehips out of their tiny pink hands. They were both wearing frilly doll's hats. Lea commented 'sweet', followed by the yellow heart emoji.

Chloe posted nudes, like Lea. She was sitting in a bubble bath with Bagel held close to her chest—staring at the camera like she was trying to seduce the person behind it. We guessed that her sister had taken the photos. Chloe had drawn black wings onto her eyes, to match Bagel's. There was a dollop of frothy, white foam on his head. He didn't seem to mind being in the water.

None of us wanted to meet Violet's tunnelweb spiders, but we agreed that the photos of them creeping around her old doll's house were up there with Lea's snake content.

Estelle told us she'd convinced one of the boys she was seeing to break into the zoo and steal her a cotton-top tamarin, or as Estelle called them, 'Those monkeys that look like David Bowie in *Labyrinth*'. Boys were always doing ridiculous things for Estelle, but this was on a new level.

'He'll get arrested,' Wallace said. 'Remember that guy who tried to steal a squirrel monkey for his girlfriend? He got two years.'

'The monkeys beat him up,' Chloe added. 'They broke his leg.'

'I think he broke his leg getting into the enclosure.'

'He had little bruises all over his back, though. And two cracked teeth.'

'What about the monkeys?'

'Two of them were injured, the rest were just freaking out.'

'It's all good,' Estelle butted in. 'This guy works there. He's got a swipe card.'

None of us were surprised when he chickened out, or when Estelle dumped him, but we didn't expect him to show up at her house with a guinea pig.

'As if that's any kind of substitute.'

Kaya had been in Japan when the pet frenzy started, but she'd witnessed it on Instagram. When she came back, she brought an albino hedgehog with her.

'That's not fair,' Chloe said. 'She already spent a whole year in Tokyo posting pictures of shrines and sky towers and stuff, why does she need to butt in on the pet thing too?'

We were all getting sick of going round to our friends' houses to visit their pets by the time Mochi arrived. We asked all the usual questions: how much did he cost ($580, plus $220 to import him into the country), what did he eat (freeze-dried mealworms), how long would he live (hopefully six years). It was hard to imagine any of us having pets for that long. In six years we could all be living in different cities. We could have babies.

We ran our hands over Mochi's prickles. Like Chin and Chilla, we found he looked disturbingly rat-like close up.

'That hedgehog is ugly as shit,' Estelle said as soon as we were out of Kaya's house. 'Those red eyes.'

Mochi only lived for a month. 'He had cancer,' Kaya told us. 'I didn't know.' She paid another $250 to get him taxidermied, and kept him in a bell jar on her desk. Not long after that, Estelle decided to sell Chin and Chilla: 'They're too expensive.' Katy confessed Roy was never hers, and Roy's actual name was Toothless, as chosen by her younger brother: the real owner. We heard from Chloe's flatmate that Bagel was spending more time at the neighbour's than at home. Lea stopped posting photos of Medusa, and when we messaged asking why, she replied, 'skin infection :('

Wallace flew back to their parents' farm for Easter, leaving us to look after Bartholomew. 'Make sure you take him on walks,' they instructed. They kissed his nose five times before they said goodbye.

Every day, we sent Wallace pictures and videos of Bartholomew to prove that he was healthy. They sent back pictures of sheep and cows.

The day before Wallace was supposed to come home, they sent a photo of something fluffy and brown, snuggled in the corner of a shoebox. It looked like a pair of cashmere socks, rolled into a ball. We zoomed in and noticed an ear, a leg. It was hard to tell if there was one creature or two curled up together. We typed a message.

what is that

It was a few minutes before Wallace replied.

friends for bartholomew

We called their phone.

'It was an Easter miracle,' Wallace said. 'We were hiding eggs in the garden for my little cousins and next minute we find these baby rabbits under the hedge.'

'So you're keeping them?'

'Yeah, in my room. I'm going to house-train them. Their names are Cinnamon and Nutmeg.'

'How are you going to bring them back on the plane?'

'In my pockets.'

We brought Chloe's cat cage with us to the airport. The cage was lined with a towel, and there was an old teddy in there too. We waited at the domestic terminal for fifteen minutes before Wallace came through the arrivals gate. They didn't wave. They walked a straight line towards us. Their eyes were red with blinked-back tears, but they were trying hard to look okay. They kept their hands locked in their jacket pockets while we hugged them. We felt their body shaking.

'Their hearts were beating so fast,' Wallace said.

BLOOD MAGIC

You only saw her at parties. Short black dress and hair straightened. Dark velvet shirt and curls tied back. Sitting on the couch, the toilet, the doorstep. Locked in conversation with a girl, two girls, a boy. That peppery Comme des Garçons perfume. Dancing in a cramped living room, eyes closed. Eyes unblinking. Offering a half-drunk bottle of red wine. Red lipstick. Lipstick smudged. Whispering in someone's ear. Hand on waist. Sneaking into a bedroom, the garden. A girl, a boy, a girl.

You had friends who'd hooked up with her. They all said it was good, really good, but they were always drunk, or on drugs, and couldn't remember exactly how it went. They remembered her knee pushed between their legs. They remembered her mouth in the dark. They remembered telling her they hadn't done this much before, and the way she said, That's fine. Everyone remembered her body. For a lot of them, she was the first girl—they didn't even think they were like that. At least two of them had boyfriends. No one regretted it.

You weren't sure what she did during the day. Someone said she worked in a library, someone else said it was a call centre.

There were rumours she used to dance at one of the clubs in town. She had a Master's in philosophy or psychology, from a university in another city. You had a feeling she'd spent her childhood in France, but it might have been somewhere else. You were sure you'd overheard her speaking in another language. You hadn't spoken to her yourself.

She was never in any of the pictures. Even when your friends got their film developed and posted long photo sets on Instagram, she didn't feature. You could look for her in the crowd and you might see curly hair or a pale arm, but it always turned out to be someone else.

That spring, there were less and less pictures. It was a pity, considering how much time you all spent getting ready. When you checked your camera roll the next morning, it was a blur of limbs and coloured lights. Your friends said their film all came out underexposed.

The same thing was happening to your memory. You woke up with bruises on your legs and hickeys on your neck and no idea how you got them. Tiny ziplock bags and lollipop sticks in your pockets. Stains on your top that looked like blood but could be red wine or cranberry juice—you weren't sure. Jaw and head aching. You took your 5-HTP and sucked on an electrolyte ice block. You called your friends and made jokes about blacking out and they said, Same. You pieced together the memories you did have: your ex telling you how good you looked tonight, that girl vomiting in the bath, noise control, a strawberry cream Chupa Chup passed in circles around the dance floor. When you mentioned the Chupa Chup, your friend gasped. She'd forgotten. That boy with the shaved head, the strawberry flavour of his mouth.

It was funny until it kept happening. It wasn't like you were drinking more than usual. You began to wonder if something was up with the drugs. They could be laced with something psychedelic, or maybe an opioid. You watched a mirrorball spin for hours, whole parties unfolding in its tiny squares of colour and light. Girls stripping down to their underwear and running their dresses under the tap. Amber-brown crystals that looked like cicada shells and tasted poisonous. A roomful of people huffing on balloons. She was always there too. Coming out of a bedroom all flushed, wiping her mouth.

Your friend started seeing auras. Yours was dark red, your other friends' were all green. Multiple people said they'd hallucinated a creature that looked like a bird, sometimes a whole flock of them. There were the usual faces melting and patterns moving on the wall. One girl was convinced she'd seen a ghost: a pale and thin woman drenched in blood, just like all the stories. She decided to take a break from partying after that.

Every week, you and your friends agreed you were going to have a chill one, then every Friday someone messaged their dealer and you all changed your minds. It was birthday season and there were at least two parties most weekends. Girls got vegan, gluten-free cakes custom-made and elaborately iced with their names on top, but by the time they cut into them, only a few guests had an appetite. A forgotten ice-cream cake melted on someone's kitchen bench. Your friend blew out his birthday candles and set the smoke alarms off.

You went to a flat warming in an apartment with no windows, and just as you were starting to roll, the music stopped playing and you were plunged into pitch black. There was a lot of screaming before everyone realised it was a power cut. Phone torches came on and someone found a Bluetooth speaker and for the rest of the night you could only just see the people in front of you. You saw her kissing a man with a beard. What happened in the dark stayed in the dark.

A girl passed out in someone's backyard, then a week later a boy was taken to the hospital. His friends said he hadn't even taken anything that night, but people got wary. You bought a testing kit. The safe colours showed up. It's something in the air, your friends said. It's the moon in Pisces. Everyone agreed their dreams were more intense than usual. You'd had sleep paralysis twice in one month, and your flatmate had a recurring nightmare about someone climbing in his bedroom window.

Halloween fell on a Saturday. Your friends wanted to go as fairy-tale characters, and because you had pale skin and dark curls, you were automatically Snow White. You tied a red ribbon into your hair and took an apple from the flat fruit bowl. You arrived with Belle. Her dress was so big you had to trail behind her like a bridesmaid, making sure it didn't drag on the pavement. She had the front hitched up with one hand, a plastic rose in the other. One of the witches smoking in the front garden stubbed out her cigarette so she could give Belle a hug, then asked where her Beast was. Belle had prepared her answer weeks ago. She brushed the rose's polyester petals against the witch's cheek.

There'll be plenty of Beasts tonight.

Half the girls inside were wearing angel wings, and you had to turn at an angle to get past them. The carpet was already littered with feathers. *Jennifer's Body* was playing through a projector onto the living room wall, without any audio. There was a bonfire in the backyard.

Goldilocks and two bears waved you over to the kitchen. They asked if you were at the Halloween party last night, and you both shook your heads. The guys at that flat were creeps—you'd saved your energy for tonight. The third bear wasn't coming because he was too hungover, Goldilocks explained. You all rolled your eyes.

Little Red Riding Hood tapped you on the shoulder and tipped her hood towards the bathroom. You and Belle followed her in. The light was so bright it made you all look tired and blotchy. Your cheeks were already pink from the wines you'd had at home, and your dress was laced up so tight all the blue veins on your chest were visible.

Snow for Snow White, said Little Red, as she fished a bag from her cloak pocket.

You each did a bump out of her long, crimson fingernail, and agreed to give it an hour before you did any more. Another three girls went into the bathroom after you.

The rush kicked in quick. Belle's eyes were as wide and unblinking as an owl's.

Little Red waved a hand in front of them. My, what big pupils you have!

Belle gave her the finger, then went over to a group of boys without costumes.

Little Red leaned towards you. What's the bet she's asking which of them is meant to be the Beast?

You danced with a group of nuns, and Morticia Addams cracked a glow stick into a bracelet for you. On the wall behind her, Jennifer was eating raw chicken out of the fridge, but people kept stepping in front of the projector and blocking her out with their shadows. Clouds of vapour filled the room and made everyone's faces hazy. You could smell menthol, undercut by a sickly medley of fruit and candy flavours. Blood pumped into your lips and palms. You ran your hands down your neck to your chest. The music was dark and synthy, with a distant screaming sound running through it. None of the songs were familiar.

In the kitchen a girl in a skeleton onesie was bobbing for apples while a crowd of zombies cheered her on. You remembered your own apple, left somewhere by the door. You wondered if anyone would pick your costume without it. Your dress was blue with the fitted bodice, but it didn't have the Disney yellow skirt.

You picked her costume immediately. She was standing in the garden: plastic tiara and white dress drenched in bright red blood. Her hair was down in its natural state. She turned and looked at you. The fire flickered between her body and yours. You had no choice but to walk over to her.

You exchanged hellos. Her accent was barely noticeable. She was just as beautiful up close. You told her you liked her costume—you'd watched *Carrie* for the first time the other day. She adjusted her tiara as she thanked you. You'd never realised how red her hair was. In the dark it looked brown, but now it was glowing like a flame. You felt your jaw clenching as you watched her. The fire was making your face hot.

She touched your cheek. Her fingers were so cold they distracted you from the gesture. Mirror mirror on the wall, she said. Who's the fairest of them all?

You were sure your cheeks had passed from Snow White's rosy blush to fully flushed. She suggested you both go inside.

The nuns were still dancing, and now some angels and the witches had joined them. When they saw you together, the angels smiled. The witches raised their eyebrows.

The two of you danced facing each other. Her eyes were closed and you knew you should close your eyes too, but you couldn't stop watching her. The strobe light pulsed from red to blue to green and her skin soaked up all of it. You wondered what highlighter she was wearing. Maybe it was some kind of dewy serum. The shimmer was so subtle you noticed it only when the light changed. She took your hands in hers and interlaced your fingers. Her hair brushed your shoulder. She moved so perfectly in time with the music, you thought she must have heard it before.

You're hot, you told her, even though she was so cold you had goosebumps up your forearms.

She opened her eyes. So are you.

The zombies took over the dance floor and you went back out to the fire. She dragged two deckchairs together and you sat talking for what could have been one hour but might have been three. You could feel the conversation getting away from you even as you spoke. You were sure she said she worked for one of the ministries, but you forgot which one. You told her about your postgrad crisis and coming out to your parents and a million other things you'd promised yourself you wouldn't talk about. She glanced at your chest and you guessed that she was looking at your veins. You noticed she didn't shave her armpits, which made you feel good about your own. When she caught you grinding your teeth, she put her finger in your mouth. It was like ice. You bit and she grinned.

Your hands are freezing, you said.

She put them between her thighs. Bad circulation.

You ended up in a bedroom with the angels—their feathered wings abandoned on the floor. They'd put on their own music and now they were all jumping on the bed. The two of you helped each other up and danced with them, your feet heavy and unsteady on the mattress. The ribbon that used to be in your hair was now tied loose round her neck, and her tiara had disappeared. When you fell down into the duvet, she fell down with you.

You were on the tail end of your period, but took your tampon out anyway. She was already sitting on your bed. You warned her about the blood and she pulled you onto her. She kissed your neck first. A gasp slipped out before you could catch it. You wanted to kiss her back, but your lips were on her forehead and the way she was sucking your jaw was leaving you incapable of anything. She bit and it hurt and it turned you on. You kept expecting her to stop, but didn't want her to.

She untied the bodice of your dress and unhooked your bra without letting her mouth leave your neck. She stopped only to pull them over your head, then her lips were on yours. She kissed like she was trying to fuse your faces together. The only way to keep your balance was to lean hard into her. Her hair and skin smelled of the smoke from the fire, and she was still so cold that when her fingers slid inside you, you sucked in your breath. The chill made you tighten. She twisted and you clenched onto her. The cold thawed and turned hot. You forgot to breathe out. She hooked into the deepest part of you and your breath came loud.

You thought about mentioning the blood again when she flipped you down and slid off your underwear. Her nails would be caked with it. You pulled off her dress and ran your hands all over her body. She looked like she'd come out of a pre-Raphaelite painting, like she'd been touched up with gloss. Her hair fell around her waist in perfect curls. You couldn't see a single spot or scar on her skin.

She tongued circles around your nipples until they were hard and all of your skin had goosebumps. She kissed your navel and you grabbed at her head. By the time she got between your legs, you were clinging to whole fistfuls of her hair. You caught a scream in your hand when you came. She

kissed the tendons on the insides of your thighs while you got
your breath back.

In the light of the bathroom, your lips and cheeks looked
stained red, and the veins on your chest were neon blue. The
hickeys would take at least a week to fade. You had faint
smudges of blood all over. You wiped at some of them while
you peed, and hoped your blood had tasted okay.

Her skin was still cool when you climbed in bed next to
her. You offered her a jumper and she said no, she'd warm up.
She lay with her arm pressed against you, and you felt the heat
from your body absorb into hers. She blinked in the dark.

The party lights flashed red, blue, red, blue. You needed to
find her. The screaming sound weaving through the music
sounded closer and more human than it had before, and the
air was so thick with vapour you couldn't recognise the people
surrounding you. Someone who wasn't quite Belle and wasn't
quite Little Red held a key up to your nostril. The gritty
powder burned and dripped a poisonous taste down the back
of your throat. Your nose was running. Blood. You pinched it
shut, but the flow was too heavy to stop. Red streamed down
your chin to your chest. Some of it got in your mouth. The
salty taste made you starving. You craved something meaty.
Blood splattered your dress, the carpet, the kitchen floor.

She was standing in front of an open fridge. Her mouth
and hands were full of raw chicken, and as you walked closer
she held some out to you. In her palm was a gory red heart.

You didn't realise you were awake until you opened your eyes
and she was looking at you. There was barely any light in the
room. It was still early morning.

I have to go.

Okay.

There was a lot of needing to leave and not leaving before she finally left. You pushed back your bedroom curtain to watch her walk down the street, but she'd already gone.

You messaged Belle and she congratulated you, then joked that sleeping with her was a rite of passage for girls in this city.

Was it as good as everyone said?

You sent her a picture of the hickeys and she replied with the skull emoji, then the spiral eyes.

When Belle called that night, you assumed she wanted details. You were confused when she asked if you'd heard about Sam.

Sleazy Sam?

I guess you don't know then.

Sam lived in the flat that had thrown the Halloween party on Friday. According to Belle's friend Izzy, the ambulance turned up around 1am. Sam was carried out on a stretcher. No one was sure exactly what had happened, but he was dead before sunrise.

Belle let out a long breath. Everyone's assuming it's drug-related, of course. I don't know how to feel about it. Obviously I didn't like Sam.

I can't believe we were partying on Saturday with no idea.

I might go with Izzy to the funeral. For moral support.

Belle would be going more out of nosiness than anything else, but you'd never call her out on it. You wanted to know too.

Belle's voice lowered. It makes you think about all those other hospitalisations, doesn't it? Apparently some boy died at a party up the coast the other month, too. And there were those deaths at the festivals.

The stuff we've been taking seems okay, though.

Maybe we've just had really good luck.

You always found Mondays the hardest. Sunday's afterglow had faded by the time your alarm went off for work. Coffee did nothing for your exhaustion, but made your hands shake and your stomach turn. Your jaw was too sore for a muesli bar and you hadn't been to the supermarket, so you settled for a mandarin and some olives. You googled a list of ministries on your phone and tried to remember which one she'd said she worked for. You narrowed it down to seven.

There were no seats left on the bus, so you had to stand. Your wet hair had soaked through the back of your shirt and made your skin crawl. You glimpsed a woman on the street with long red curls and craned your neck to see if it was her. It wasn't, and on closer inspection her hair was more brown.

This happened twice more throughout the day. Every time someone walked into the shop, you geared yourself up for it to be her, though you couldn't imagine her buying organic groceries anyway.

By the afternoon you were so tired that you considered telling your manager that a friend had died on the weekend and you needed to go home. You went to the bathroom instead. You took your phone out of your pocket and prayed for a notification from her, even though this was incredibly unlikely. You'd never seen her on any social media. Your screen showed a series of messages from Belle, an email from Student Job Search, and a text from an unknown number. You read it without breathing.

—

184

The second time cut your lip and bruised your neck. It tasted like salt. She dripped blood into your mouth and got stains on your white T-shirt. You had to soak it for a whole day.

The third time, she whispered she'd missed you and you whispered it back. You made each other come more times than you could count. Every time you looked at her, you were shocked by how beautiful she was. You're killing me, you said.

The fourth time, you couldn't stop staring at each other. You'd never looked at anyone's face this much during sex; usually you avoided eye contact. You fell asleep with your head on her chest. Her heart was too soft to hear.

You called Belle and she was shocked. Neither of you knew anyone who'd slept with her more than once. You had no idea how you'd done it. Belle pointed out that you'd been on your period the first time: it's blood magic. Have sex with someone while you're on your period and they're always obsessed with you. Belle asked if you were dating and you said you wouldn't call it that. She only came over at night; you didn't go on dates. Belle was unimpressed.

She doesn't take you out in public? Red flag. You haven't been to her place? Red flag. She's always busy during the day? Red flag.

Your phone was getting sweaty in your hand. Can we talk about something else, please?

Belle didn't have much to report from Sam's funeral. All the boys cried, the speeches sounded a lot like the ones at his twenty-first, an Ed Sheeran song played. She still wasn't sure how he'd died—his family and friends avoided mentioning it. Some people were saying he'd had a health condition. Most people were saying there's some dodgy stuff going around right now. Better be careful.

Scattered images played across your mind as you fell asleep. Fish-shaped soy sauce bottles filled with clear liquid. Squeezed into drinks or under the tongue, like medicine from a dropper. Soap taste. Your body sank into the couch, next to a blurry, passed out figure. Up near the ceiling, dark bird-like shapes nestled together. Your eyes wouldn't focus, and your limbs were heavy. The person next to you slumped against your shoulder and you tried to push them off, but your body was sluggish and moved only in slow motion. Their head rolled to the side, and you realised it was Sam. Blood trickled from his nose. Your screams came out as whispers.

Suddenly her arms were around you and she was pulling you up, out of the nightmare. She stroked your hair and told you over and over it was just a dream, it was just a dream.

You didn't mind taking a break from partying. She was all the serotonin you needed. You went to work with barely any sleep and a high-neck top to cover the marks on your neck. Your manager asked if there was any reason you were smiling so much today and you played dumb, but felt your face turn red. You wiped counters and shelved gluten-free pasta. Daytime was a waiting zone. Even when you were serving customers, she was in the back of your mind.

You pictured her sitting at a desk in front of a computer. It didn't look right. You found it difficult to see how she'd fit into an office setting. You imagined her in the staff room, microwaving leftovers. Swiping her access card for the lift. None of it was convincing. You tried to imagine how her co-workers saw her. Older women probably wished she'd wear more clothes. Some of the men would have asked her out for a drink, you were sure. You wanted to be a fly on the wall.

Your lack of sleep caught up with you by the afternoon. You wondered how she was coping—at least your job was mindless. Your phone buzzed in your pocket while you were cashing up, and you rushed to check it as soon as you were done.

Free tonight?

You replied immediately.

The vegetables you'd bought earlier in the week needed using, but you only had the energy for toast. She always came over after dinner, which was a relief. Your cooking was sketchy at the best of times, and her IBS meant there was a long list of things she couldn't eat.

You fell asleep on the couch and woke up with just enough time to tidy your room and get changed. You tried on two jumpers and fixed your hair, then shut the wardrobe door so your mirror was out of sight. The last thing you wanted was to see your own reflection while you were fucking.

Your flatmates were out, so you could be as loud as you liked. Having sex with her was like entering another dimension. Time lost its usual meaning. It was impossible to guess how many minutes—or more likely, hours—would have passed before you reached over to check your phone. You said and did things you never would have thought outside of this zone, and when you recalled them afterwards, they seemed like something you'd dreamed or watched in a movie. Her staring at you, then squeezing her eyes shut and shaking her head like she couldn't believe it. Your whole body too sensitive to touch. Her leaning forward to say, You're the best sex I've ever had. You could only remember these highlights—the rest was sealed off and impossible to access once was the sex was over.

Half of your bed was on the floor and your hair was damp. She wasn't sweaty at all. You asked how and she shrugged. Her index finger traced the web of veins on your chest. When she got to the bruises on your neck, she apologised. You told her you liked them, but she still looked worried. You pushed back your hair to show her the scar at the corner of your forehead, where your younger brother threw a glass at you. She pressed her lips to it, then pulled your hand towards her heart, so you could feel her concave chest. You ran your fingers back and forth over the dip.

Tell me something else I don't know about you.

She laughed and looked at the door. What do you want to know?

Anything. I don't mind.

She hummed and scratched the back of her neck.

You laughed. Where did you grow up? I know you told me on Halloween, but my memory's blurry.

She was born in a city you'd never heard of, but recognised as European. She couldn't remember much about living there anyway. She'd never stayed in one place for long. Her best friends all lived out of town or overseas. You asked about her family, and she told you she didn't have much of a relationship with them these days. You were on shaky terms with your own parents and knew not to press it. It was obvious that she was uncomfortable talking about herself. You apologised for being nosey and she shook her head. Keep asking.

Sometime between three and four, conversation trickled out and you fell asleep. You were always the first to drop off, and she was always the first to wake up. You watched her crawl out of bed and pull on her work clothes. The sun wasn't even up. You whispered a goodbye and she slid her hand between your legs for a second. When you begged her to stay longer, she motioned a stab in the heart.

You lost count of these nights. Her long red hairs turned up in your sheets and the bedroom carpet. The sex got better and better.

No matter how tired you were during the day, your exhaustion disappeared when you were with her. You complimented each other back and forth for hours and swapped endless questions. Sometimes her answers were vague or elusive. There seemed to be a lot from her past that she couldn't remember clearly. You knew there were things she hadn't told you yet, and you didn't want to rush her. You listened carefully. Your notes app was full of things she had said that you didn't want to forget.

Childhood fears—the dentist, dogs.

Never learned to swim.

Watch: A Girl Walks Home Alone at Night.

You memorised her body. She didn't have any stretch marks and never bruised. Her teeth were the only thing about her face that wasn't perfect. She had the sharpest canines you'd ever seen, and a small gap in the front—not wide enough to be fashionable, but wide enough to notice. She had no distinct smell, aside from the woody traces of perfume that lingered on her collarbone and wrists. All her clothes smelled of this. When she went away for a weekend, you slept with her shirt.

Your period marked a month since Halloween. You tried not to think about the fact that it also marked a month since Sam's death. You'd been having more nightmares than ever before. She often woke you up from them. You didn't tell her what the dreams were about. Belle had sent you a post about a guy who'd gone missing from a party down south, and you still hadn't replied. It gave you a queasy feeling that you couldn't totally explain.

You'd been dead tired for the past few days, and it felt good to blame PMS rather than your late nights with her. She didn't get her period. It wasn't birth control, and she'd assured you she ate enough. A couple of your friends' periods had mysteriously disappeared too, around the end of last year. They'd joked it was all the partying.

You didn't bother warning her about the blood this time. She got on her knees and pushed your skirt up over her head as soon as you closed your bedroom door. She touched the pale green tampon string.

A month? Feels longer.

I know, it's crazy.

It's nice.

You fucked against the wall, then on the floor until your knees had carpet burn. She passed you water and covered you with the duvet once you'd cooled down.

I want every month to be like this.

As soon as she said it, she touched the wooden bed frame. You pulled her hand to your mouth and kissed the knuckles.

Me too. I just wish we had endless time. We need three extra hours every day for talking, another three for sex, at least two for movies . . .

She pressed the pad of her finger against your cheekbone and lifted a stray eyelash. Wish for it.

You smiled at her, then blew the eyelash into your bedroom.

The exhaustion didn't go away with your period. As days went by, you became more and more drained. You phoned in sick, just to lie in bed and sleep. Belle called twice in the afternoon, then three times in a row that evening. You answered.

Finally. Where are you?

In bed.

With her?

No, she's got a birthday out of town this weekend.

Good. Can I come over? I have tea.

There was no use arguing. You dragged yourself out of bed and into your clothes. The room smelled of sex, and there were blood stains on your sheets. Belle couldn't come in here.

Her knock was so loud that you and your flatmate both swore. He guessed it was Belle before you had time to warn him. You opened the front door. Belle's face screwed up.

You look like death.

Thanks.

She sat at the kitchen table and asked what you'd been up to, but she was looking at your flatmate's back. She couldn't talk to you properly until he'd left the room. You offered her a hot drink, which she declined. Your flatmate finished his meal prep and started wiping down the bench. You sat down at the table, across from Belle. This felt oddly formal. You wished you had something to do with your hands.

Belle folded her arms. No one's seen you in ages.

Your flatmate hung the dishcloth over the tap and left the room. Belle checked he'd closed the door, then turned again to you. She'd been messaging a guy she met at the funeral. He said Sam had died of hypovolemic shock, which—according to her research—could be caused by a large number of things, including a burst aneurysm, stomach ulcers, or too much sweating and throwing up. Belle was still figuring out its connection to drugs. All this had inspired her to message her cousin up the coast about the guy who died back in August. He said it was definitely a drug thing. The guy sold GHB. Date rape.

Your head was starting to hurt. You stood up to get a glass of water, but your vision went black and you had to sit back down. Belle asked if you were okay, and you told her you needed to go to bed.

You should see a doctor. The bags under your eyes are insane.

She patted you on the shoulder as she left.

You pulled the duvet over your head and thought about Halloween. You were wearing your Snow White costume again, and she was *Carrie*, but you were dancing far closer this time. A huge mirrorball was spinning directly above you. She said something in your ear, and you asked her to repeat it. The music kept drowning her out. Finally, you heard her words.

I need to tell you something.

There was a shattering sound, and you instinctively put your head down. You felt the tiny shards of glass splinter into your skin and catch in your hair. When you dared to open your eyes, you were alone in your room.

The only doctor available at short notice was a man. It was over a year since you'd last had an appointment, so you had to answer a lot of questions about medication and birth control. You hadn't been on the pill since you were a teenager; it made you depressed. No, there wasn't a chance you were pregnant. Yes, you'd had multiple sexual partners since your last visit. Male and female. Not always protected. Only one partner in the last two months. Female. He asked if you knew when her last sexual health check was. You shook your head.

The doctor weighed you and measured you and checked your blood pressure. He made a concerned humming sound

when he read the gauge, which immediately caused your
heart to speed up. Your blood pressure was very low. He asked
about your symptoms: fatigue, weakness, low temperature.
Periods: regular, usually light. Diet: vegetarian for five years
now. He nodded and printed out a prescription for iron and
B12. You needed a blood test and an STI swab.

She came to yours as soon as she got back to the city. It was
just three days since you'd last seen each other, but it felt like
weeks. She was already grinning when you opened the door.
Her hair was redder than you remembered, and her eyes were
greyer than the green you'd imagined while you were apart.
You hugged and her smell gave you a headrush. When she
kissed you, it felt like the first time all over again: her cold
lips, the metallic taste of her mouth.

You asked about the birthday party and her time away. She
made a face. She hadn't really wanted to go, but knew she had
to. She was more worried than you'd expected when you told
her about the doctors. She touched the shadows under your
eyes and asked when you'd get the results back from your
blood test. You weren't sure. She checked your temperature
with the back of her hand, then pressed her fingers against
the pulse in your neck.

Maybe I should let you rest for a few nights.

Do you want to?

She held your gaze, then shook her head.

You climbed onto her lap and pushed her hair back from
her face. She was even paler than you were.

I don't want to wear you out.

You lifted her arm and kissed the soft spot inside her
elbow. The concern didn't leave her eyes. You kissed up to her
wrist, then her palm, then slid her middle and index finger

into your mouth. She tipped her head back so you could see her whole neck. You watched her mouth open and eyes close. The smell of her breath was addictive. She got her free hand between your legs and past the elastic of your underwear. You could feel yourself slipping into the zone. She pulled away long enough for you to take off each other's clothes. You pressed your lips to her skin. The chill of it still amazed you. She pushed her fingers between your legs and you did the same. Your bodies mirrored. You stared so hard into each other's eyes that neither of you remembered to blink. Her hand gripped your forearm. You could tell she was close, and this brought you closer too, until you were gasping into each other's mouths, so the sound wouldn't wake up your flatmates.

She kissed your neck so hard it hurt, but in an exhilarating way. You were too light-headed to open your eyes. Before you could kiss her back, she turned your body so you were facing away from her. She kissed down your spine, and slid her hands around your chest, then down your stomach and between your legs again. The sensation was so intense your eyes shot open.

It took you longer than it should have to process what you saw. Things weren't how you expected. Usually, your wardrobe was kept closed, but tonight you'd left it open, revealing the mirror inside the door. You were reflected in it. Your eyes automatically squeezed shut, like you'd looked at the sun. When they opened, what you saw was the same. You were on the bed, naked, kneeling. Alone.

Everything blurred. Your ears were ringing. Her hands reached for you and your body jumped away. There were tears on your face. She was crying too. You couldn't process any of her words. Her mouth was on your ear, then there were footsteps, a door clicking shut.

As soon as she was gone, you wanted her to come back. You called out her name, but there was no response. Your body wouldn't stop shaking. The humming sound was so loud you wondered if it could be coming from your speakers, or something in the wall. You were overtired, you were overtired, you were overtired. You shut the wardrobe door without looking at the mirror.

Your phone buzzed. You answered so quickly you didn't read the caller ID.

Thank god you picked up. I have the biggest tea.

Belle. I can't really talk right now.

Fine, I'll summarise. So you know that guy I've been messaging? I just left his house. He was telling me about the night Sam died. Guess who Sam was with the last time they all saw him.

I don't know.

Your new girlfriend. They were making out in the bathroom. Then, like, an hour later, Sam's flatmate found him passed out on his bed.

Your body went still. Belle was saying something about dehydration and blood loss. You covered the receiver. There was a shuffling sound. At first it seemed to be coming from the hallway, then you heard a rustle outside. You moved towards the window. Shadows rippled on the gauze curtains.

*

You only see them at parties. Hand in hand and matching dark clothes. A shared tote bag. Emerging from the bathroom with untucked shirts and messy hair. Whispers. Secret code. Fixing each other's eyeliner, dress strap, back zip. Cornered

by some boy. Slurred questions. Sisters? No. Threesomes?
Raised eyebrows. A locked door. Muffled shouts. Slipping out
through the window and onto the fire escape. Kissing with
stained mouths. A blur of black and red. The sound of sirens.

MANIFESTO

My friends put stickers over their laptop cameras, but not me. I don't mind if someone is watching. I keep my social media profiles public in the hope that someone will look. I leave my curtains open while I get changed, and close them when it's too dark for anyone to see inside. What a waste it is that no one gets to see me looking so lovely all the time. My hair always dries in perfect ringlets when I'm alone.

I leave the door to my wardrobe open—all my colour-coordinated clothes on display. I keep my prettiest lingerie out in vintage baskets. I buy myself red roses to sit on my dresser, then hang them on the wall to dry. I face all my Virgin Mary figurines towards the bed so that when I sleep I feel like they are watching me. Such wonderful things deserve to be seen.

*

When my grandma shared the story of how she and my grandad got together, she told me, *There is nothing more romantic than feeling a man's eyes watching you and following you in the streets.* I laughed and told her he should have been arrested, but I know what she means. I don't mind when people stare. There is a part of me that enjoys being yelled and whistled at. I was secretly excited when a homeless man accosted me in front of my crush, asking, *Doesn't she have a beautiful smile? She should be a film star!*

*

Since I was a teenager, I have imagined my life as a movie. I am constantly watching myself from inside the screen. At fifteen my favourite movies were *Titanic* and *Romeo + Juliet*. My favourite singer was Lana Del Rey. Every time I went to a bookshop, or the library, or used public transport, all I thought about was whether someone was about to fall in love with me. When my family and I caught the Cook Strait ferry, I would dress up to stand on the top deck and stare out to sea—waiting for my romantic lead to appear.

I went to my friend's sixteenth birthday as an angel, even though I knew no Romeos would be invited. Sometime in the night, I went downstairs to text my sister. When I turned to leave the room, the girl who would soon be my best friend was standing in the doorway with her camera held up to her face. We stayed up all night, talking about the meaninglessness of life, and agreed that the most important thing was to enjoy it as much as possible.

She posted the photo on my timeline a week later. I'm smiling at the ground—feathered wings just poking out above my shoulders. I immediately made it my profile picture. It was the first photo of me that I really liked.

*

At the auditions for a school play, I met a boy who looked like a young Leonardo DiCaprio. My best friend agreed. He and I were cast as the couple that everyone else wanted to be. Rehearsals were twice a week, but I seemed to bump into him everywhere I went: the movies, the waterfront, the bus stop. I began imagining myself through his eyes instead of just my own. My clothes took on a new magic. My perfume smelled like a secret. Everything I did became beautiful. Reading in bed at 1am was beautiful. My fingers grasping the yellow pole on the bus were beautiful. Battling my bedsheets in the wind that whipped the washing line was beautiful. I knew he didn't love me back—I doubt he even thought about me—but when he left the city my screen went black. I started to shrink.

My best friend was the only light. We both knew we were stars. We always said life felt like a movie when we were together. Our mothers joked that we were like the *Heavenly Creatures* girls. My best friend insisted she was the pretty one, and I accepted. She told me my clothes looked better on her than they did on me, and I accepted that too, though I cried about it when I was alone.

We only ever kissed in the dark, and we never said we were in love with each other. We said we were in love with 'us'.

*

After years of waiting, I met a boy who saw me exactly how I wanted to be seen. He called me angelic, mysterious, beautiful. He made jokes about how tiny I was in comparison with him. I quickly fell in love with the way people saw us together. I loved feeling like a prize he had won, like a catch he had caught. I loved meeting him at the gates of my all-girls school while all the girls stared. I loved that everyone knew automatically that I'd lost my virginity. I loved being told we were the hottest couple at the party, the cutest couple at the ball. I loved when his friends took me aside and thanked me for how happy I had made him. I loved joking that I was his manic pixie dream girl.

Eventually I fell in love with him too. The more time we spent together, the less I cared how he saw me. We slept in the same bed every night and told each other every thought we had throughout the day. Three years flashed by. He began spending most of his days at home—a supporting role in my life rather than the lead of his own. The way people saw us felt less and less true. My life with him didn't feel like a movie. Every time I drank gin, I would end up crying about this to a group of friends. I always woke up embarrassed. I wished I could delete the whole scene. My friends told me not to worry: *You look so pretty when you cry; you should do it all the time.*

After I broke up with the boy, I barely cried at all. When I did, I tried to catch my reflection. The tears always stopped before I could.

*

I was already falling in love with someone new. When I told my friends about them, I had to hold myself back from saying all the dumb lines: *I've never felt like this before, we had this instant connection, it's opposites attract.* I knew that dating them would be a nightmare—they could barely reply to a text—but I was obsessed with the idea of us together. I was obsessed with our matching pale skin and dark hair, our matching heights. The alliteration of our names. I was obsessed with our contrasting clothes, our incompatible birth charts. I was obsessed with introducing them to everyone in my life, and being introduced to everyone in theirs. How easily we all got along. I was obsessed with how surprised all my friends would be if the two of us actually worked out.

When I looked in the mirror, I imagined how they would see me rather than how I saw myself. I wore all my most romantic clothing, and made sure never to repeat outfits. I bought new perfume. I kept my skin so soft I couldn't stop touching it. I curled my eyelashes and applied nude eyeliner to my waterline, so I looked awake even when I'd been up all night thinking about them.

There were only ever two photos taken of us together, and I look bad in both. I look good in photos taken minutes later, with only me in them. We were at the beach. I was wearing white silk shorts—pink and yellow flowers tucked in my hair.

I was wearing a beach dress made of blue towelette when I told them I liked them. They put their hands on their cheeks and thanked me, then said they needed to go home and think. I took a picture of myself lying on my bedroom carpet after they left, then sent it to all my friends to show them how pink my cheeks were. In the photo my eyes are bright and dewy. I'm glowing.

We spent a lot of time talking about movies, and a lot of time analysing each other. They told me they wished they had some of my confidence, my self-assurance.

You seem confident, I told them.

They shook their head. *No, you're the kind of person you walk past in the supermarket and think 'She's confident'. I'm not like that.*

I had to admit this was probably true.

We talked about our star signs, our enneagrams, our

numerology, our birth cards. Mine were Strength and The Star. *That's accurate,* they said. Theirs were The Empress and The World, which I thought were better than mine, but they didn't like them at all.

I lent them poetry collections and they lent me books about the psychology of love. Every week, they would come over to my house and we would tell each other what we thought. We barely ever liked the same parts.

Some of the ideas I just don't relate to, I told them. *Like that chapter where he's saying when we're in love, we admire and idealise that person so much we feel inferior, like we're not good enough for them. That whole 'I love another and so I hate myself' idea. Then if they like us back, we think 'Why? If this person is as incredible as I thought, they wouldn't have the bad taste to like me.' So we stop liking them. See, I don't feel that at all. I feel the opposite.*

I already knew from the amused smile on their face that this was the chapter they related to the most.

They called me beautiful once. It was while we were kissing, which also happened only one time.

They came round to my house almost every week for a year. They had seen me wear all my clothes at least once, many of them twice. Usually I made sure to get home hours before they came over, so I would have time to wash and dry my hair, but that Wednesday I only had time to put on a fresh top. It was red, with tiny pointelle hearts. My mascara had been on for more than eight hours.

When they arrived, we went up to my room and sat on my bed, as we always did. They told me I was pretty and hot and smart, but they just weren't attracted to me. They said my knowing that I was pretty and hot and smart was the reason why.

As soon as I shut the front door behind them, I started to cry. The playlist I had put on before they came over was still playing. I sobbed through a whole song before I thought of looking at myself in the mirror. My eyes were bloodshot and my nose was running. *My friends were lying*, I thought. I went into my flatmate's room and cried in her bed while she patted my hair and told me, *They're a weirdo, they give me the creeps.*

When I felt better, we sat on the couch eating buttered rēwena bread. She made me laugh—joking about her addiction to checking herself out in reflective surfaces, including the kettle at work. I brought out strawberry-scented facial spray and make-up wipes for us to clean off our mascara.

By the way, she said. *Has anyone ever told you you're pretty when you cry?*

SCHOOL SPIRIT

It was important that we broke into Erskine College on a full moon. It was in Cancer, which wasn't ideal: we didn't want anyone crying. Also I was on my period. But it was a Saturday night and none of us had work the next morning, which was too rare an occasion to pass up.

Saffron and Frances got to mine at 10pm. I had been waiting since 9:30—the time we had agreed upon.

'What took you so long?' I asked, opening the back door of the car. 'Oh, hello.'

A girl with very pale skin smiled at me nervously from the other end of the back seat. 'I'm Olivia. I'm a friend of Saffron's.'

'Right. I'm Meg.' I got in and slammed the door. As far as I knew, Saffron didn't have any friends outside of our extended circles. I suspected she'd met Olivia on Tinder.

'Olivia studies fine arts.' Frances turned to pass me an open packet of Oreos.

'Nice.' I took one of the biscuits and split it so I could see its white circle of icing. 'I've been craving sugar all day.'

Frances raised an eyebrow. 'Period? Same with me and Saffron.'

'Witch bitches.' I laughed. 'We're all synced up with the full moon.'

I took another Oreo then offered them to Olivia. She shook her head. I thought about asking if she was on her period too, but decided I better not.

'Can someone feed me an Oreo?' Saffron asked, not taking her eyes off the road. I passed them back to Frances and watched her put one in Saffron's mouth.

'Have you been to Erskine before, Olivia?' Frances asked.

'No, I'm from Christchurch.'

'None of us have been either. But Saffy's done lots of research.'

Frances was the only person who called Saffron Saffy. Occasionally I slipped and called her Saffy too, but it sounded wrong coming out of my mouth.

Olivia shifted the tote bag in her lap. It was one of those black ones with the white square on it. 'Are you all from Wellington?'

'Only Meg,' said Frances. 'Saffron and I are from New Plymouth. We've been friends since high school.'

I met Frances in first-year psychology—which we both dropped—then met Saffron at Frances's birthday party. Saffron and I hooked up that night, and at a few parties after that, but over the past year our flirting had mostly steadied into friendship.

'Is the moon out yet?' Saffron asked.

I peered out the window. 'I think the clouds are hiding it.'

'It's in Cancer, right? That's no fun.'

'Olivia, what sign are you?' Frances asked.

'Um, Pisces?'

'Uh oh,' Saffron and I said in perfect sync. She spun her head round to grin at me.

Olivia looked scared. 'What's so bad about Pisces?'

'They're our least favourite sign,' I said. 'But maybe you'll be an exception.'

'What's the rest of your chart?' Frances asked.

'I don't know.'

Frances and Saffron glanced at each other. 'Not even your moon? Your rising?'

'I'm not sure what time I was born.'

'Text your mum and find out,' Frances said.

Olivia obediently got out her phone. 'I'll text my dad.'

None of us said anything while she tapped on the screen. I felt somewhat sorry for her, but I was mostly annoyed at Saffron for inviting her along. The three of us had been planning this night for months.

'Here we are.' Saffron pointed up the hill at a cluster of large Gothic buildings.

Frances peered at them. 'So old-fashioned.'

The largest building was four storeys high, with a wide balcony attached to each level. The balconies' white railings stood out in the dark.

'They look so out of place,' I said. 'Like a blip in time.'

'They'll be knocked down soon.' Saffron turned onto a road leading up the hill. 'So we better get a good look tonight.'

*

Let me tell you what I remember. Steep steps and dark trees dripping. Slipping on the slick and avoiding the cracks, afraid of breaking my mother's back. The smell of pine needles and rain. Magpies squawking. I remember looming buildings, though they loomed less over the years.

A labyrinth of long corridors. Gleaming floors. The smell

of polish and beeswax. I remember the ringing of the bells. A chorus of footsteps. Two rows of girls, the Mistress of Discipline close behind. A whisper, then the sharp crack of her wooden clapper: Silence, ladies!

I remember brown pinafores in winter and green pinafores in summer. White uniforms on Feast Days. White veils for the Procession of the Lilies. A flower placed before the statue of our Lady, in the Black Forest Grotto. Mary, I give thee the lily of my heart. Be thou its guardian forever. I remember curtsying for Reverend Mother—quick curtsy in the corridors, deep curtsy at assembly. Gloved hands fumbling with holy pictures. Needlework classes on Saturday mornings. Standing on the grille to feel the waves of hot air up our skirts—forbidden, but everybody did it. Art books with pages glued together to hide the male nudes. Rumours of a headless nun in the piano cells. Birthday flowers from Best Friend.

I remember pressing glasses against closed doors. Gruff voices on the radio. Ships and submarines. I remember girls arriving from far away. Extra prayers at assembly. A black plane overhead. Girls crying and what is happening what is happening. Two girls taken into Sister Caldwell's office to read a letter from their mother.

I remember waiting for Sister Hayes to think we were asleep. Listening to the click-click of her heels as she walked from the dormitory to her room. Pulling back the curtains between our cubicles and climbing into Best Friend's bed. Hushed voices washing in and over each other. I remember voices disappearing.

*

Saffron parked at the bottom of a tall grassy slope. There was fencing up around it, but other people had broken in before us, leaving a convenient hole in the wiring. We eased through it one by one. The slope was rutted and tangled with weeds, which made it easier to climb but took focus to navigate. Frances and I were nearly at the top when we heard a yelp from behind us. I knew immediately it was Olivia.

'You all right?' Frances yelled.

'Yeah, I think I just twisted my ankle a bit.'

Frances and I looked at Saffron. She sighed and began climbing back down the slope.

'See you up there!' I yelled. Frances and I scurried to the top, her leather satchel bumping repeatedly against her hip until she grabbed it with her hands instead. We ran to the chapel as soon as we were on the flat, and collapsed, laughing, outside the main door.

'Sappho strikes again?'

Saffron had made her Tinder bio 'you can call me sappho' back in first year, and this is how we had referred to her Tinder personality ever since. Her nickname in our group chat was 'sappho the serial dater'. Saffron pretended to be embarrassed, but it was obvious she enjoyed it.

'Sappho extreme. She forgot they had a date planned tonight.'

'Typical.'

'Such a dick. She didn't even say sorry, she just texted Olivia back like, "Want to come ghost-hunting?"'

'Did she tell her we were coming too?'

'Well, you'd think so, but then we pick this poor girl up and she's obviously completely confused as to what I'm doing in the car.'

'No way.'

'And Saffy barely said a word to her the whole car ride.'

'I can't believe she's a Pisces. She does seem kind of wimpy.'

'For sure, not Saffy's type at all.'

'And how does she not know her birth chart? I thought all gays were into astrology.'

'Same. She did look cute in her Tinder pictures, though.'

The two of them walked towards us—Olivia limping a little. Her body leaned to the left, weighed down by the tote bag hanging off her shoulder. I wondered why she hadn't left it in the car.

'Let's go round the back,' Saffron said. 'Apparently there are windows you can climb through.'

The chapel itself was intimidatingly tall. The windows were stained-glass, with pictures of what I assumed were Jesus and Mary, but it was too dark to see, and they were so high only birds could reach them. Behind the chapel, a smaller building was attached. None of the windows had any glass left in them and most were boarded up, but Saffron soon found a low window where the boards had begun to rot away. She took a jumper out of her backpack and wrapped it around her hand, then pushed hard on what was left of the boards. They fell apart easily. The rest of us helped brush away the splinters, clearing the sill. Saffron swung her leg over and straddled the sill awkwardly while she bent her head and shoulders into the room, then whipped her other leg over and dropped inside. Frances and I did the same, and helped Olivia in after us.

Inside was even darker than I had expected. Saffron brought out a large yellow flashlight and the rest of us turned our phone torches on. At either side of the chapel entrance were two stone basins with leaves and roses carved into them. Saffron dipped her fingers into a basin then quickly pulled them out. She shuddered as she shook off the droplets. 'That is not holy water.' Frances passed her the jumper, and she wiped her hands. We stepped into the chapel.

The first thing I saw was all the glass. Light glinted off the floor in a splintered mosaic of shattered bottles and windowpanes. Most of the glass was clear or dark green, but there were reds and oranges and even some blues. Amid all the glass was a lot of bird poo, some empty spray-paint cans and an abandoned cardigan. Most of the pews were intact. I looked up. The ceilings were so high the light from my phone couldn't reach them: above the stained-glass windows, everything dissolved into darkness. Saffron scanned the lower part of the walls with her torch. They were almost completely covered in graffiti, most of it tags or drawings of dicks. Up near the altar were the remnants of a fire and some empty chip packets. I wandered over to a smashed statue and crouched down to pick up a white stone finger only a little smaller than my pinkie. I put it in my pocket.

'Hey Frances, it's you.' Saffron was pointing her torch at one of the pictures on the wall. 'Saint Francis.'

Frances and I looked up at the painting. It was about the size of an old TV screen and framed in wood, with three little crosses sticking up at the top. 'Where does it say Francis?' I asked.

'It doesn't. You can tell because he's got a wolf.' Saffron moved her torch along to the next painting. 'And that one's Genevieve because she's holding a candle.'

I pointed my phone light at Saffron. 'I forget you grew up Catholic.'

'So do I.' She smiled, but I could see her chewing the insides of her mouth. 'Block that shit out.'

Frances opened her leather satchel and got out her camera, looping the strap round her neck. She snapped a photo of me before I registered what she was doing.

'Delete that.'

She stuck her tongue out and turned to take a picture of one of the windows. The camera flash was offensively loud in the quiet chapel. Frances stepped into the confessional, then poked her head back out. 'So, is this place actually haunted?'

'People on the internet say it is,' Saffron said. 'One of the nuns died in the study room, back in the thirties. And they used to have funerals in here.'

I sat down in one of the pews. Olivia sat behind me.

I turned round. 'Did your dad reply?'

'Oh, um . . .' She checked her phone. 'I was born around 3pm.'

'You should do your chart now.'

Olivia opened Google. I watched Saffron. She had climbed right up onto the altar and was taking a close look at everything. She picked up a thick white candle from the cluster arranged around a worn-out Virgin Mary. Frances snapped a picture and Saffron's head shot up, grinning.

Olivia coughed. 'I'm a Cancer rising?'

Saffron sniggered. I was surprised she could hear us from up on the altar. 'Pisces sun and a Cancer rising, oh dear.'

'What's wrong with it?'

'Nothing,' Frances said. 'It's just double water, lots of emotions. Your rising is how you come across on the surface, so it's not that important. Your moon is the interesting one. It's like your inner self—mood and feelings and all that.'

'It says Virgo.'

I laughed. 'Damn, what a chart.'

'I'm a Virgo moon too,' Frances said. 'Wouldn't recommend.'

'It's the source of all her anxiety,' I added.

211

'What signs are you guys?' Olivia asked.

Frances sat down next to me, her legs stretched out over my lap. 'Meg's a Capricorn.'

'What does that mean?'

Frances smirked. 'It means she's heartless.'

I punched her shoulder. 'I have a heart! Saffron's the one with an Aquarius moon.'

Saffron hopped off the altar. 'Never felt a feeling in my life.'

'Saffy's a Sagittarius rising, so she seems all chaotic and fun,' explained Frances.

'But don't let it mislead you, I'm actually very serious.'

Olivia was looking at Frances and me. Frances grinned and rolled her eyes.

There was a soft, tearing sound. I looked around for the source. Saffron's mouth had fallen open and her eyes were locked on the altar. I turned towards it. A small flame quivered on one of the candles.

'Did one of you do that?' Olivia's voice was quivering even more than the flame.

'Nope,' said Saffron. 'That's some supernatural shit.'

She rushed back up onto the altar and leaned close to look at it. I couldn't tell if she was faking or not. It was the kind of prank she would play, though I had no idea how she'd have done it. She flicked her pinkie through the flame, back and forth, then pinched it between two fingers. Frances took pictures from multiple angles.

'Can we go somewhere else?' Olivia asked.

I waited for Frances to answer, but she was too focused on the photos. 'In a minute,' I said.

*

I remember the first half of that year in pinks and blues. I was a senior and had finally been awarded a ribbon: dark blue, draped over the shoulder, tied loose at the waist. Best Friend was the highest blue ribbon—Head Girl. Her hair was long and black, but when it caught the light it glinted almost navy. The best-behaved juniors were given pink bows, then pink ribbons. Pink cakes were served for afternoon tea. Best Friend and I delivered buns to the pink and blue rooms of the infirmary. Little blue lamps lit the chapel altar every evening.

It was my and Best Friend's honourable charge to be sacristan. We spent an hour each day down on our hands and knees cleaning. The smell of oil and incense lingered on our clothes and in our hair. All the girls were jealous.

While we cleaned, we talked about Altar Boy. My Altar Boy was different to Best Friend's Altar Boy. We didn't know either of their names. We had only ever glimpsed the boys out of dormitory windows, or from a distance at the Procession of Christ the King. We knew there was a girl who had sent letters back and forth with her Altar Boy, but Best Friend and I would never have taken that risk. We would've lost our blue ribbons if we were caught. The girl and her boy got away with it by replacing his name with a girl's name, so when the nuns read over the letters they assumed she was writing to her sister or a friend.

Best Friend had a sister once, but she'd died in the earthquake. The earthquake had killed a lot of people in the town Best Friend came from. Here, all we'd felt was a ripple. Best Friend's parents sent her here straight after the funeral. She was seven. Her sister had been eleven. Best Friend never told me her sister's name, but sometimes I saw her flinch when Sophie was called on the roll.

*

In the week before the Feast of the Sacred Heart, we spent even more time in the chapel than usual. We gathered Lily of the Valley and filled the pews with their scent, saving a few to press inside the Bible we kept next to our bed. We arranged candles in the shape of a large heart, beginning on the altar and trickling down the steps. The evening before the feast, each girl was given a candle with a thick paper cover for the Procession of the Lanterns. Symbols of the Sacred Heart and Mother Mary were cut out of the paper covers in sharp snips. The chapel was dark. Rows of girls wove in and out of the benches, singing hymns in French, then English.

> A message from the Sacred Heart;
> What may its message be?
> 'My child, my child, give Me your heart
> My Heart has bled for thee.'

*

There was no missing the moon when we got back outside. The clouds had cleared just enough for it to take its place in the sky: dramatically bright. Frances and I spun around in circles, throwing our hands up towards it. Saffron howled like a werewolf. Olivia kept her arms folded tight across her chest.

'Now the real magic can happen!' Frances cupped her hands round her mouth and called out towards the college, 'You can come out now, ghosts!'

Olivia looked alarmed, but I wasn't sure if that was because of the way we were acting or the possibility of encountering an actual ghost. She gazed down the hill to where the car was parked.

'Take a photo of me, Frances!' Saffron held her hand up like a crab claw. 'So it looks like I'm holding the moon in my fingers.'

Frances held the camera up. 'It's just a bright circle. You can barely tell it's the moon.'

'Do it anyway.'

Frances took a few steps back, then shuffled to the left. 'Your hand needs to be higher.' She gave Saffron more directions, then started laughing. 'This is impossible, I'm just going to take it.' The camera snap, snap, snapped.

I peered over Frances's shoulder while she clicked through the photos. The moon was slightly out of Saffron's reach in all of them, but she was grinning as if she'd caught it.

'You look so sweet, Saffy,' I said. Blood rushed to my cheeks as soon as I registered the slip. No one else seemed to notice. Frances zoomed in on Saffron's face, making the three of us laugh. Olivia made no move to come look at the photos.

We checked multiple doors to the main building before we found one with a broken lock. It looked like someone had smashed it with a hammer. A red sign titled 'EARTHQUAKE PRONE BUILDING—DO NOT APPROACH' was taped at eye level.

It was easier to see inside this building than it had been in the chapel: none of the windows had curtains, and they let in enough light that we barely needed torches. A cage elevator cast criss-crossed shadows on the floor.

Saffron yanked the elevator's gate open, and we all flinched at its screeching cry. She stuck her head inside but kept her feet firmly planted in the corridor. 'What a deathtrap.'

I traced my finger along a cross carved into the staircase pillar. It seemed there were crosses carved into every possible surface of this building, both outside and inside. I'd even seen little crosses on the peaks of the roof.

We headed up the stairs and into one of the classrooms. It was long empty of desks or a blackboard, but there was a large pile of wooden planks in the middle of the room.

'It looks like someone was planning a bonfire,' Frances said.

I nudged one of the planks with my foot. 'Or a sacrifice.'

Olivia sat on the windowsill and rubbed her ankle. I wondered why she didn't ask to go and sit in the car. I would have suggested it, but I couldn't think of a polite way to bring it up.

This room had even more graffiti on the walls than in the chapel. Saffron put down her flashlight and picked two spray cans off the ground. She shook them. One still had a bit of paint left in it. She aimed the nozzle at a blank space on the wall and a white blob formed. She kept going until the blob was shaped more like an ice block.

'It's a ghost!' She dropped the cans and picked up her flashlight again, shining it at the ghost-blob. Frances snapped a picture.

I laughed. 'Would she get into art school, Olivia?'

I turned my torch in Olivia's direction and saw the glisten of held-back tears in her eyes. She forced a smile. 'Ha ha, maybe.'

Everyone laughed except Olivia. She really was acting like a Pisces.

'I'm thinking about Miss Gates, Saffy.' Frances was taking pictures out the window now. The view was all dark suburbia. A wispy cloud was lit up almost gold as it stretched across the moon.

'When are we not thinking about Miss Gates.'

'Is this the one that was always going on about school spirit?' I asked.

'Show some school spirit, girls!' Saffron spoke in a posh accent, though it wasn't clear which country it was supposed to be from. 'She wouldn't even let us sit with our friends in class. It wasn't school spirit.'

'She was fully crazy. She had this thing about hair.' Frances put the lens cap back on her camera.

'She made everyone put their hair up in a bun before they came into the classroom,' Saffron explained. 'She couldn't even deal with plaits, it freaked her out.'

'Why?'

'I don't know, nits or something. OCD.'

'And then.' Frances folded her arms. 'Saffy came up with this idea.'

'It wasn't completely my idea. Rosa Martin was the one who said we should leave a lock of hair on her desk.'

'Yeah, but you were the one who convinced the whole class to cut some off.'

I rolled my eyes, but I couldn't keep the grin off my face. 'You haven't changed, Saff.'

Saffron was grinning now too. 'We arranged the hair from lightest to darkest. It looked really cool. You have photos right, Frances?'

'Yeah, on my laptop. But honestly, guys, you should have seen Miss Gates's reaction. She fully started crying, in front of the whole class. Her entire body was shaking.'

Saffron giggled. 'And then she had a nervous breakdown and quit her job.'

'No way.'

'Yep.'

I laughed, kicking one of the wooden planks. Olivia was

silent. I looked at her, trying to convey with my eyes that she was free to go back to the car, if she wanted to. She forced another smile.

Saffron and I led the way back down the corridor while Frances and Olivia trailed behind. We stuck our heads into every doorway, though most of the rooms looked much like the one we'd just been in. Frances gasped when we came to a room with a little stage in it. The backdrop had been painted to look like the countryside, but had clearly been done by teenagers. The hills were lopsided, and the school girls climbing up to the top were smudgy and spaced out at such a distance they barely looked like a group.

'There's four of them.' Frances climbed onto the stage and began taking photos again. 'Like us.'

Olivia sat down on a bench that was pushed against the wall and got out her phone. Her sore foot stayed on the ground but the other one jiggled frantically. Her nervousness was so palpable it almost made me nervous. 'It's nearly midnight,' she said.

'The witching hour.' Frances turned and took a photo of Saffron and me standing in the doorway.

'I thought the witching hour was 3am,' Saffron said.

'Are you guys planning on staying here that late?' Olivia's foot jiggling intensified. I stared at it, as if staring could force her to stop.

Saffron shrugged. 'If we feel like it.'

Frances hopped off the stage. 'You two come stand up here, be my models.'

We obeyed. For the first round of photos, Frances had us stand back to back in the centre of the stage, facing out into the wings.

'Stop hunching, Saff.'

I felt Saffron's back straighten. Her shoulder blades nudged into mine. I wondered if she registered this too. Unlike Frances and me, Saffron and I almost never touched. It was one of the few unspoken rules that had arisen after we'd stopped hooking up—as if the slightest physical contact could lead to us fucking again. The two of us stood statue-still while the camera snapped and flashed, snapped and flashed.

'All right, now turn around so you're facing.'

When we turned, our faces were ridiculously close. Saffron jutted her neck out so our noses bumped and we both started giggling.

'Behave yourselves,' Frances ordered, and we both stared at the ground, like kids who'd been told off.

'Get closer.' We shuffled forward so the toes of our shoes were almost touching. Both of us were wearing Docs: Saffron's were Oxfords and mine were Mary Janes.

'Heads up,' Frances directed. 'Look at each other.'

We lifted our faces carefully. Our mouths were so close, it was impossible not to think about kissing. I tried to force the thought from my mind, worried that some random impulse would take hold of me and I'd actually do it. I'd felt this impulse at least once with most of my friends, but it was more dangerous with Saffron. It was strange to think how well I'd known her mouth. Her lips were in a funny, pouting position that meant she was trying not to laugh. I racked my brain for something serious. My face settled into a blank. The camera flashed in the corner of my eye and I tried not to wince. Gradually, Saffron's face relaxed to match mine. I had thought her face was the most beautiful face I'd ever seen back when I had a crush on her, but now it seemed mostly ordinary. I could recognise its flaws as flaws rather than endearing imperfections. We stared at each other. Her eyes slowly turned from sources of meaning to circles of colour and black. It scared me how vacant they were: just body parts, blinking mechanically. I had no idea what was going on behind them.

'Done. Thanks guys.'

We stepped apart as Frances jumped back onto the stage. Saffron instantly came back to life: her eyes full of spark again. I wandered over to Olivia and took a seat. She quickly exited out of Google Maps.

'Give us a show,' I called out to Saffron and Frances. They rolled their eyes. 'Come on, you were both in school plays weren't you?'

'Only one.' Frances put on a high-pitched warble. 'Double, double, toil and trouble!'

'Fire burn and cauldron bubble!'

They both started laughing at such a hysterical volume it sounded like they were still playing witches. Saffron spun in a circle then stopped, swaying.

'I thought you said there were four girls.' She pointed at the stage backdrop, still giggling. 'There's only three.'

Frances looked at the painting again. 'I swear there were four. I must be losing my mind.'

I frowned. 'I thought I saw four too.'

Saffron threw her arms up in delight. 'We're all losing our minds!'

'Check the photos,' I said. I rushed up to Frances so I could see the camera screen. She flicked back through, then zoomed. Our voices were soft and in sync. 'Fuck.'

Saffron hurried over and looked at the screen. She looked at the painting. 'Okay, that's scary.'

A phone started ringing and we all jumped. The ringtone

was unfamiliar, but we all checked our phones anyway.

'Hello?' It was Olivia's phone.

The three of us breathed out. Frances turned her camera off.

'Oh no, okay. Hang on.' Olivia put her phone down and looked at Saffron. 'My flatmate's locked out.'

'Oh,' Saffron said. She sounded unimpressed.

'She needs me to let her in.'

'Can she go wait somewhere?'

Olivia spoke into the phone. Her voice was awkward and uncertain. She turned back to us. 'She said she'll wait in McDonald's.'

'All right. We'll try and hurry then, I guess.'

Olivia said 'Love you' before she hung up. She stood. 'Okay, we're going?'

'Once we've finished looking, yeah.'

Olivia faltered. 'Huh?'

'There's still heaps of rooms we haven't seen,' Saffron said. 'We'll just do a quick look.'

Tears were brimming in Olivia's eyes again. I resisted the urge to roll mine.

'But . . . I need to let my flatmate in?'

A suggestion hovered on the tip of my tongue. 'Maybe you should call an Uber?'

'It's a sixty-dollar fare.'

I raised my eyebrows. Of course she'd already looked.

'I don't want to be in here,' Frances said. 'I'm going to wait in that classroom.'

For a moment, I thought Olivia might break down crying. I tensed, ready to respond. She swallowed. 'I'll wait with you,' she said to Frances.

*

I remember so much silence, and so many sounds. The scritch-scritch of pencils during study in the library. A class down the corridor speaking French in unison. Mother Nottingham's raspy breathing. I remember the static of cicadas, calling us outside on summer afternoons. The sound made us fidget in our seats. A girl tapped her foot until the table shook. Best Friend tensed up. Her eyes darted around until they met mine. I smiled. Her body calmed.

We prepared for our first communion with a three-day retreat. None of us were allowed to speak. It made everything feel like a dream: we were dizzy with silence. Our desks were all turned towards the wall and decorated with holy cards and treasures. A visiting priest read us passages from *The Lives of the Saints*. We couldn't figure out if the stories were true or not.

Talking during meals was allowed on very special occasions. Sometimes Reverend Mother read to us from the pulpit, but most days a bell rang out until the dining hall was silent. Best Friend and I sat at different tables, each responsible for maintaining a group of juniors' dining etiquette. We taught the girls not to ask for things like butter or salt, but to offer them to others in the expectation they'd be offered back. The food was always awful: a grey sludge of porridge for breakfast, a grey sludge of something dead for dinner. We taught the girls not to complain. This rule was cast aside when we were served boiled tripe. Even Reverend Mother apologised. The local fish-and-chip shop received the biggest order they'd ever had.

All day we looked forward to afternoon tea. Sometimes it was bread and jam, sometimes it was sugar buns. One time it was afghans the size of our outstretched hands.

After the black plane, there were no afghans and no sugar

buns. The jam was spread extra thin. Even the juniors knew not to say anything.

*

It was much more exciting with just Saffron and me exploring. Every time I remembered the painting, I felt a rush of adrenalin. A good kind of fear pumped through my body.

'The candle in the chapel,' I said. 'Was that you?'

She looked confused. 'What do you mean?'

Another rush of adrenalin. 'I guess not.'

We arrived at a closed door. Words were printed in French on a panel above it.

'Salle d'études,' Saffron pronounced. 'Study room. This is where that nun died.'

She gave the door a push, but it didn't open. I couldn't tell if I felt disappointed or relieved.

We made our way along the corridor until we found the bathrooms. Two long rows of mint-green basins were lined up back to back, the mirrors above them lined up too. The mirrors were covered in grime and the few patches of reflective surface had been written on in marker. CELESTE & EVE <3 2016. VM & HER HEAVENLY ANGELS, G & A. ADA WAS HERE. The basins were littered with chocolate wrappers and cigarette butts. Someone had left an old rain jacket on the ground.

Saffron twisted one of the taps, but no water flowed. 'It's good to get away from all . . .' She waved her hand at the doorway. 'That.'

I laughed. 'You invited her.'

She made a face. 'I didn't know she'd be so . . .'

'Watery?'

'Yeah, anxious energy. It's draining.'

'It's her chart, it's not her fault.'

'Mmm. I should have asked what sign she was before I asked her out.'

She dug a Sharpie out of her backpack pocket and started writing in the bottom corner of a mirror. S—A—P—P—H—O. 'Aren't Pisces supposed to be into astrology and the occult and everything?' she continued. 'She seems so anti all of it, why would you come ghost-hunting if you're not into ghosts?' She passed me the pen. I drew a star, then wrote M—E—G, followed by another star. Saffron perched on the edge of a basin. She sighed. 'I swear every Pisces I've ever met has a victim complex.'

I turned to her and raised my eyebrows. 'Olivia must be having a pretty shit night, to be fair.'

I wasn't sure why I was defending her, but disagreeing with Saffron felt good. I handed the pen back to her and our hands touched. We locked eyes. Something clicked. Disagreeing with Saffron felt good because it felt like flirting.

She rested the pen on the side of the basin, then grimaced. She pushed her fists into her stomach. 'Do you have any painkillers?'

I dug around in my jacket pockets. My hand clasped something cold and hard. I pulled out the stone finger.

'What's that?' She leaned close, touching it with her own finger. I watched her admire it.

'You should have it.' The words left my mouth before I knew if I wanted to say them, but when she grinned I was sure.

'Actually?'

'Yeah, you brought us here.'

Saffron thanked me and put the finger in her backpack pocket.

I turned back to the mirror and started drawing the Capricorn symbol. 'I used to wish my parents would send me to boarding school.'

'Why?'

'I just liked how it seemed in books and movies. I probably would have hated it.'

Saffron's reflection shuffled in the mirror as she nodded her head, mottling around the patches of rust and mildew. 'My parents wanted to send me to boarding school.'

'Really?' I faced her again.

'In year eleven. It was a Catholic school, like here. They thought it would . . .' She laughed. Her eyes followed her foot, drawing circles on the ground. 'Straighten me out.'

This surprised me. 'Were you a bad girl, Saffron?'

She laughed again. 'No, they thought it would . . . make me straight.'

'Oh.' I laughed too. 'Teenage girls locked up in isolation from boys—the perfect place to be straightened.'

'Yes. They clicked on that eventually.'

We were both silent. I wanted to ask more, but I didn't want Saffron to feel uncomfortable. She barely ever spoke about this stuff.

She ran her finger along the basin edge. 'Do you believe in ghosts?'

'Isn't that the whole reason we're here?'

She shrugged. 'I don't know if I really believe, though. Sometimes I feel like I'm pretending—to myself, I mean.'

'I get it. Even with the full moon. Sometimes I'm looking at it and it's like I'm pretending I feel this intense feeling, but really I just think it looks pretty.'

Saffron laughed. 'I hope ghosts are real, though. I want to believe.'

'Me too. If I saw a ghost, my life would be complete.'

Her expression turned sneaky.

I stared at her. 'What?'

She stepped towards me, almost as close as when Frances had been taking photos. She turned her head and looked right into the mirror. 'Bloody Mary, bloody Mary, bloody—'

I clamped my hand over her mouth. 'Don't you dare, Saffy.' I coughed. 'Saffron.'

She peeled my fingers away to speak. 'You can call me Saffy.' My hand stayed awkwardly close to her face, her fingers clasped loose around mine. Her expression was still sneaky. Kiss, said a voice in my head, immediately followed by a No no no no no no. I knew in my body that I didn't really want to, but it was like I'd been possessed by some kind of demon, a stirrer-spirit, urging me to make trouble. If Saffron made a move, I doubted I'd be able to resist.

In the silence, I noticed a gentle jingling. I glanced away from Saffron to look at the mirrors, and saw they were moving just enough to bump into each other. Our reflections wobbled like water. She noticed too.

'Is that the wind?'

We looked at the windows. They were all shut. A sick feeling rose into the back of my throat. The mirrors shook like something was threatening to break out of them. My hand gripped Saffron's and hers gripped back. The adrenalin pumping around my body froze into fear: there was no faking any feeling now.

*

I remember my hair was wet that night. It was winter and the water made my ears cold. We were allowed three baths a week. Other days, we carried basins of water back to our dormitory cubicles and washed behind the curtains we had each pleated when we'd moved in. Wednesday was a bath day.

Before bathing, we polished the dormitory floor with tea leaves and wax, sweeping up with brooms that stood taller than we did. Mother Nottingham watched to make sure we polished right into the corners. The floors became so shiny we could almost see ourselves reflected in the wood. Our arms ached.

We took hot water bottles to bed. Best Friend and I pushed the curtain between our alcoves back just enough to see each other. We made faces until lights out.

I thought about Altar Boy until I fell asleep. I didn't dream of him. I dreamed of black planes and the radio rumbling. Something dropped. I woke up to shouts and pitch dark. My bed sloshed from side to side. Cupboard doors swung open, Bibles crashed to the floor. A water jug smashed into pieces.

'Stay in bed, girls!' It was Mother Nottingham. I had never heard her voice so shrill.

A junior screamed from across the corridor. I could hear Mother Nottingham pulling at the light switch, but the lights did not come on.

'Sing the school song, girls! As children of the Sacred Heart . . .'

Some girls joined in with shaky voices for the second line. The room shook around us.

> We'll strive till death to do our part
> Storms may gather on our way
> But we'll be loyal to Island Bay.

The shaking stopped halfway through the chorus. I looked for Best Friend, but the space beyond the alcove curtain was empty. As the hymn finished, I heard girls creep out of their beds. I got up and slipped past the curtain to where Best Friend slept. She wasn't there. Something touched my ankle and I almost cried out, before realising Best Friend was hiding under the bed. She didn't look like Best Friend. Usually I felt younger than her, but now I felt much, much older. I took her hands and helped her out, then we walked towards the girls gathered at the windows. The city was a shadowy blur. The streetlights had gone out, and no light shone from any of the houses.

Aftershocks continued to startle us till morning. Best Friend stayed in my bed, gripping my wrist tight every time the room quaked. Nobody slept. For months we were woken around 2am each night by a jolt in the earth. Even after the aftershocks stopped I woke at 2am, certain that something was shaking.

*

The floor shifted beneath us and we both swore, dropping to the ground. The room swayed with the familiar rhythms of an earthquake. There was nothing to hide under, so I put my head down and covered it with my arms. Saffron did the same. I pressed my forehead to the floor. It shuddered and heaved. I heard things falling and breaking in other rooms.

The quaking continued inside my body even after the room stilled. It took a little while to realise I was the one shaking, not the ground. I kept my arms over my head.

'I think it's over.' Saffron sounded disturbingly calm. 'We need to get out of here. There'll probably be aftershocks. This building is red-stickered.'

She was already standing by the time I looked up.

I wanted to stay close to the ground, but embarrassment pulled me to my feet. 'That was big, right?'

'You should know, you're the Wellingtonian.'

'It felt longer than other earthquakes.'

Saffron nodded, but didn't look so sure. We stood an awkward distance apart. The moments before the earthquake felt faraway, imagined.

A mirror that had been propped against the corridor wall had fallen and smashed in silver splinters across the floorboards.

'Seven years' bad luck.' Saffron cleared a path with the toe of her shoe. I stepped after her.

We called Frances's name three times before she stepped out of a room across the corridor. Olivia's tote bag was hanging on her shoulder, along with her leather satchel. I'd never seen Frances look so out of it. A large bump was swelling fast on her forehead, and Saffron and I both rushed to her. 'Shit, are you okay?'

She touched her hand to the bump. 'I'm a bit spinny.'

Saffron put her arm around Frances's waist and shifted the tote bag onto her own shoulder. 'You might have concussion.'

'No, that's not it . . .' Frances shook her head, her fingers still hovering over her face.

'We should take you to a doctor,' Saffron said.

I nodded. 'Where's Olivia?' She'd better not have hurt her other foot. We'd have a hard time carrying both her and Frances down to the car.

Frances looked at me. 'That's what I mean. Where's Olivia?'

'Is she hurt?'

Frances went back to shaking her head. 'She's not there. She's gone.'

'What?' Saffron and I looked at each other. She mouthed 'Hospital' and I nodded.

'Let's sit you down, Frances.' Saffron led her over to the wall. She turned to me. 'I should probably stay with her. Can you go find Olivia?'

I nodded and ducked into the room Frances had come out of. Some shelves and a painting had fallen from the wall, but aside from that the room was empty. I checked the nearby rooms and called Olivia's name. My voice echoed. I was starting to feel nauseous.

I went back to the others. They were sitting together on the floor and Frances was shaking her head again. 'She was in there with me, then something hit my head and I covered my face and she wasn't there anymore.'

'That's weird.' Saffron sounded confused but not concerned. This calmed my own panic a little.

'I didn't explain it right,' Frances said. 'I closed my eyes for a second, and then she wasn't there. Like, she disappeared.'

'We better call her.' Saffron got out her phone, and I checked the nearby rooms again. There was a bobby pin on the floor, but it could have been there for years.

'The phone line's down,' Saffron called out.

I stepped back into the corridor. Olivia's tote bag sat slumped against the wall. 'Don't you think it's weird that she'd leave this?'

Saffron looked at the bag too. The white square stared at us.

A ripple passed through the building.

'Aftershock,' said Saffron, before the word could form in my mind. She was already on her feet. 'We need to get out.'

'But we need to find Olivia,' I said.

'Go then.' The harshness in her voice surprised me. I felt a brief flash of hurt. 'Hurry.'

I rushed from room to room again, shouting Olivia's name over and over. The corridors all looked the same. They made me feel light-headed. When I was sure I'd looked everywhere upstairs, I ran downstairs and repeated the process. I moved even faster down there. Even though I knew Frances and Saffron were only a floor above, I was scared to be alone. My hopes of encountering a ghost had transformed into a genuine terror: every time I stepped into a room, I was sure something was going to grab me from behind the door, or slam it behind me. There was more furniture in these rooms, and a lot of cobwebs. One room had a piano in it. I crept further in and peered behind an old couch in case Olivia was hiding. The floor jerked violently under my feet. I yelped and grabbed onto the couch arm, just catching my balance. The room rocked. I looked around, unsure of whether to stay or run. A dark shape moved in the corner. I bolted. My feet flew up the stairs, too fast to feel whether the shaking had stopped. I pulled to a halt when I reached the others. 'I can't find her.'

Frances looked less out of it now. Her face was full of fear. 'Guys, I know I sound crazy but it really was like she disappeared. She was definitely in the room with me.'

Saffron still didn't look scared, but she did look stressed. 'We need to get out. We can't be in this building.'

I took a deep breath and yelled. 'Olivia!'

Frances shook her head. 'She's gone, I swear.'

I stared at Saffron, and Saffron stared at me. This was nothing like it had been in the bathrooms.

'We need to leave.'

'Without Olivia? What if she's hurt?'

'You would have found her.'

'I should check the rooms again. I might have missed one.'

'We have to get out. And we should take Frances to the hospital.'

'Do you really think she's got concussion?'

'I think I'm fine,' Frances cut in.

No one said anything. The building rattled in the wind.

'We're going.' Saffron hooked Frances's satchel onto her shoulder and passed me the tote bag. None of us looked at each other.

*

I remember the weeks following the earthquake. We all had trouble sleeping, but Best Friend barely slept at all. She didn't like to be inside. Because she was Head Girl, she and I were allowed the use of Reverend Mother's Garden. We spent our free time doing roly-polys down the sloping lawn, hopping back onto our feet and brushing the grass off our skirts when the juniors came past. Sometimes we crawled all the way up to Spion Kop. On a clear day, you could see across the sea to the South Island. We always slid back down the slope, though Reverend Mother scolded us for the grass stains on our uniforms. We took care to wash them out.

Best Friend was always tired by the afternoon. We lay on hot pine needles, soaking up the sun and sometimes falling asleep. She slept better outside than in bed at night. If the grass was wet, we'd go to the tennis courts or the cricket pitch. If it was raining, we took shelter in the Bunnyhole and watched younger girls practise their rollerskating. If the Armchair was free, we'd sit there, but that was everyone's favourite spot and hardly ever empty. You could talk privately in the Armchair: a flowery snug set into the bank, with a wooden table and seats. No one could eavesdrop unnoticed.

On the warmest days, Reverend Mother sent us down to the beach at Island Bay. We were allowed enough time in the water to swim out to the island and back. Best Friend stayed on the shore. She spent more time in the sun than anyone, but her skin got paler and paler.

Reverend Mother asked us both to decorate the Black Forest Grotto for the procession honouring our Lady of Lourdes. We trailed our hands in the fishpond and arranged flowers around the Virgin Mary's feet. On the night of the procession, we all knelt at the grotto and prayed for safety during earthquakes. We followed the procession with a bonfire on the hills. Best Friend looked almost translucent in the flames.

The second earthquake was on a Sunday. It shook us from our sleep, but we'd all been dreaming of earthquakes so much it was hard to tell if the shaking was real. Something smacked and shattered. We jolted awake. I jumped out of my bed and rushed through to Best Friend's. It was empty. I dropped to the floor. She wasn't underneath. She wasn't anywhere.

*

Getting Frances down the hill was more difficult than expected. I hadn't really believed she was concussed until I saw her try to walk. Even with us holding her up, she kept stumbling. The moon had disappeared again, and we didn't have enough hands for a torch, so for much of the walk we couldn't really see where we were going. My arms tired out before we made it halfway.

'Can we take a break?' I asked.

Saffron stopped and looked around. There was nothing

nearby that could fall on us. 'Okay.'

We sat down on the grass. My hands were like jelly.

'We should call the police,' I said. 'To report Olivia missing.'

Neither Frances or Saffron said anything. I could feel the guilt pulsing off all of us.

'We could get arrested,' I added.

Saffron shrugged. 'The phone line's down.'

'It might be better now.'

She slid her phone out of her pocket. 'What do I say?'

'Just say what happened.'

'It's going to sound like we made it up.'

'It doesn't matter.'

'Do you think we'll get in trouble for trespassing?'

'It doesn't matter.'

Saffron hesitated, then dialled 1-1-1. A pre-recorded message asked her if she wanted the police, the fire department or an ambulance, then she was put on hold.

Olivia's tote bag was in my lap. I wanted to look inside, but didn't want to be the one to suggest it. I stared at the white square. I had always assumed it was some famous painting, since all the art students I knew had one. I wondered now if it was just a label. The white looked like it had been spray-painted around a square-shaped stencil. It was dead black in the middle.

Frances drooped against my shoulder. I nudged her back into a sitting position.

'We should get you to the car,' I said.

Saffron hung up and pocketed her phone, clearly relieved. We hoisted Frances up and continued down the hill.

'What are we going to do about Olivia's flatmate?' Frances asked. 'They're going to be stuck at McDonald's all night.'

'There's nothing we can do,' Saffron said, a little too quickly. 'We just need to pretend this whole thing never happened.'

I stared at Saffron, trying to figure out whether she really believed herself. Her expression was cold, but her cheek was sucked in, which meant she was chewing the inside of it. We arrived at the car in silence.

'What took you so long?'

We all stopped.

Olivia was brushing grass off her pants, like she'd just stood up. She noticed the tote bag and reached out to take it, thanking me. 'I rushed out so fast I didn't realise.' She clutched it close to her. Her eyes were hopeful. 'We're going now?'

We stared at her like she was a ghost. She looked more alive than she had all night: her hair had been messed up by the wind and her cheeks were red. She was pretty. If she'd looked like this in her Tinder profile, I would have swiped right too. Saffron gave a zombie-nod, then fumbled in her backpack, finding her keys.

The two of us helped Frances into the front seat and did up her seatbelt. Olivia got in the back. The three of us kept glancing at her. I still couldn't believe she was real.

'You're not allowed to fall asleep, okay?' Saffron adjusted Frances's seat so she was sitting up as straight as possible.

'I'm not concussed. It's just shock.'

I got in next to Olivia. It was as if I'd just woken up from a bad dream: I felt relieved, but the guilt from before still clung to me. I had to keep reminding myself that we didn't need to drive to the police station. Saffron turned on the radio and clicked until she found a station that wasn't static. I expected a news reporter's voice to fill the car, telling us where the earthquake was centred and what it had scored on the Richter scale, but a song was playing instead. It sounded older than my parents: I didn't recognise it. We listened in silence.

When we got to McDonald's, Olivia thanked us and got out of the car. We never saw her again.

Notes and Acknowledgements

'Girls in the Tunnel' uses facts about the life and death of Phyllis Symons sourced from the National Library of New Zealand newspaper archives (Papers Past).

'Moral Delinquency in Children and Adolescents' takes its title from the Mazengarb Report of 1954 (*Report of the Special Committee on Moral Delinquency in Children and Adolescents*). Redmer Yska's *All Shook Up: The Flash Bodgie and the Rise of the New Zealand Teenager in the Fifties* and Chris Brickell's *Teenagers: The Rise of Youth Culture in New Zealand* were invaluable sources of information and inspiration.

'School Spirit' includes many stories and details from *Erskine College of the Sacred Heart, 1905–1985: The Seed Never Sees the Flower* by Sister Marie Kennedy.

*

Stories from this collection have been previously published in *The Pantograph Punch, Stasis, Turbine* and *Middle Distance: Long Stories of Aotearoa New Zealand*. Thank you to the editors.

Thanks to my first readers, the MA class of 2020, and the IIML staff. Thanks especially to Emily for believing in this book, and for being an icon.

238

Thanks to Fergus, Ashleigh, Craig, Tayi and the rest of the team at THWUP for making this book happen. Lorry for editing with such care. Tracey for the encouraging words.

Thanks to Lily Paris West for the gorgeous cover, and Ebony Lamb for the incredible author photos.

Thanks to Kōtuku for your constant wisdom and kindness. Linda for being my second mum, and for throwing immaculate parties.

Thanks to Wai, the Libra that started it all. Sinead, my first literary friend—you're my favourite Empress and my favourite Fool. Ellen for always being so Lana Del Rey vinyl. Bre for the letters and the phone calls. Thanks to Emma, Vita, Olly and Andrew.

Thanks to Maddison—you're at the heart of this book.

Thanks to Maia for sharing your chocolate coffee beans with me, and everything since.

Thanks to my family for the songs, the stories and the love. Dad for transcribing my first 'book'. Mum for the notes in my lunchbox. Faith for the beautiful embroidery on this book's cover, and for being my perfect little sister.

And thanks to Tessa—my real-life dream girl.